Blind Man's Drum

BLIND MAN'S DRUM

TOM BENTLEY

thistledown press

Canadian Cataloguing in Publication Data

Bentley, Tom, 1947 –
Blind man's drum

ISBN 1-894345-41-X
I. Title.
PS8553.E579B54 2002   C813'.6   C2002-910324-X
PR9199.4.B46B54 2002

Cover and book design by Jackie Forrie
Typeset by Thistledown Press Ltd.
Printed and bound in Canada by AGMV Marquis

Thistledown Press Ltd.
633 Main Street
Saskatoon, Saskatchewan
S7H 0J8

Thistledown Press gratefully acknowledges the financial assistance of the
Canada Council for the Arts, the Saskatchewan Arts Board, and the Government
of Canada through the Book Publishing Industry Development Program for its
publishing program.

ACKNOWLEDGEMENTS

Tom Bentley wishes to thank his editor, Rod MacIntyre, for his great generosity and insight, and Don Kerr for his ongoing support and advice.

He also wishes to thank Pat and Miranda for their love and encouragement as he abandoned the tried and true in order to embark on a creative reinvention of himself.

Although *Blind Man's Drum* is set in a real place and time, and is inspired by growing up in a small Saskatchewan community, the incidents and characters are the product of the author's imagination.

CONTENTS

Blind Man's Drum *is dedicated to the author's grandparents, the people of Biggar, and to the late Saskatchewan poet, Anne Szumigalski.*

In the middle of the Canadian prairies in the province of Saskatchewan, there is a small town called Biggar. On the outskirts of town on the side of the highway a sign states NEW YORK IS BIG BUT THIS IS BIGGAR. Most people drive past. They know little about the town. But they remember the sign.

— T.B.

CHICKEN BLOOD

Robert sat on the edge of the bathtub holding his roll of toilet paper, waiting for the blood. His grandfather slapped the straight razor up and down against the leather belt. The stropping sound stung the boy with excitement. It was much better than being in Sunday school colouring pictures of holy things.

Robert went to the Presbyterian Church once. Gladys Potts took him along after convincing his grandmother that his spiritual education wasn't up to snuff. He liked all the decorations but wondered why the church needed such a high roof. When it was time for the sermon, the children went to the basement with a Sunday-school teacher to get little drawings to put crayons on and learn about Jesus. There was a photograph of Jesus on the wall. He had blond hair, red lips, rosy cheeks and looked like a woman with a beard. If that's the son, Robert thought, I wonder what the daughter looks like?

When Will Coutts found out his grandson had been in church with that Mrs. Potts bitch, Robert's spiritual education came to an abrupt halt. So every Sunday morning after that Robert had to stay home and help his grandfather with his weekly shave.

Robert felt nervous today though. It was Monday morning. His grandfather had never shaved on a Monday. He shaved on Sunday. What if his grandfather shaved differently on a Monday? Or what if the toilet paper dropped from his hands and bounced over and landed on the cellar door?

In the middle of the bathroom floor was a heavy hinged door. Down below was a ladder that dropped straight into a dirt cellar full of coal and potatoes and chicken blood.

His grandfather had brought a chicken home once. He carried it into the bathroom and put its head on a block of wood that he'd brought in from his wheelbarrow. He clamped the head with one hand and yanked the screeching bird away from its head, squeezing and stretching its body from between his knees. After rubbing his fingers up and down the bony neck, he took his knife from his overalls and sawed through to the block of wood. He cut the chicken's head off. Right off. And the head stayed in the bathroom as the chicken ran all through the house. With no head. His grandfather couldn't chase after the chicken body because Will Coutts couldn't see. He had to wait until the chicken body ran back into the bathroom to find its chicken head. And it did. And it died. Right there with its head on top of the cellar door. Robert ran out to puke on the caragana bushes outside the front screen door.

He spent the rest of the afternoon killing Koreans on Billy Palmer's woodpile but when Billy's mum wouldn't invite Robert for supper he had to go home. He looked into the bathroom but saw no sign of the chicken body or the chicken head. He figured maybe the chicken blood had leaked through the hinges of the cellar door and sunk into the coal and potatoes. He decided he'd never step on that cellar door again. Or eat potatoes.

Robert held on tightly to the toilet paper waiting to do his duty, hoping that his grandfather didn't feel as nervous as he did. Today was different. Today was Monday. There was no room for mistakes.

Will Coutts turned on the tap and undid his overalls so they could drop to his waist. He took two white facecloths and soaked them in the stream of very hot water. He brought a chair in from the kitchen, sat down in front of the sink, and stirred with his hard-bristled brush, dropping beads of water onto the bar of shaving soap inside a bowl. Like an alchemist, Will Coutts' slow roundabout motion began to transform the unyielding yellow mass into lush and gentle fog banks. The steam from the sink began to fill the room and Robert felt intoxicated with the softness of the world. He loved the wet magic of his grandfather's incantations. He loved his grandfather.

Will Coutts towered six feet above the horizon as he pushed his wheelbarrow, guiding his memory through the streets of Biggar, Saskatchewan. He'd been totally blind in one eye for years and the other had a cataract that made it hard for him to see anything but shadows. A doctor in Saskatoon told him he could go to Rochester, New York, to have the cataract removed. Will was pretty close to going several times but always changed his mind at the last moment. Now his eyesight was so bad he thought it might be his last chance.

The smell of soap filled the bathroom as the swelling foam began to drift off the ancient medicine bowl, surrendering to the alchemist's touch.

Robert's grandmother stood in the kitchen adjacent to the bathroom chewing the left side of her lip. She stood paralysed with confusion and dread. Usually at this time of the day on a Monday morning she was in full battle with the tight suck pull of the wringer washing machine in the corner of the kitchen. Will Coutts had finally caved in and installed plumbing — the last house on the block to take the plunge. He left the outhouses out back though, just as a precaution. Who knew if those fancy pipes could stand the test of time?

For a few months after the installation, Flo was happy. A toilet, a bathtub and even a kitchen sink with hot water! It was a pity all seven children had left home and couldn't enjoy the luxury of the whole thing. Now it was just her husband and grandson. The old man slept in the back bedroom with the boy, and she in the front off the living room. They met in the kitchen at twelve o'clock for lunch and five o'clock for supper. That was it. That was the routine. And that suited her just fine.

Flo chewed her lip. Monday was her laundry day and having the old man in the house was very unnerving. She held onto the kitchen sink and breathed heavily. She didn't know if she was more afraid of him going to Rochester or chickening out and not going at all. A week without the old man would be grand. But she worried about him returning to peer beyond the shadows of his eye and seeing her two hundred and fifty pounds of rolling flesh in all its glory. She knew his blindness and was comforted by it. It gave her room to live in her own shadows. She stood frozen, breathing heavily, knowing the Happy Gang would be "KNOCK KNOCK KNOCKING" on the radio by now. She hated her sisters for making her marry the old man in the first place. "WHO'S THERE KNOCKING? . . . DA . . . DA . . . DADA . . . IT'S THE HAPPY GANG . . . WELL COME ON IN!"

Will Coutts lifted the two scalding cloths from the sink and let them fall onto his face as he leaned his head back against the chair. Robert breathed into the mist cloud and said a silent goodbye to the comfort of the swimming eye — a pale blue sun through the fog-bank whiteness, veiled and oozing wide to the back of the head, promising that the universe goes on forever. There are things in this world you can't even imagine, his grandfather always said.

The old man leaned forward to let the white mask drop from his face and onto the edge of the sink. He pulled his full mane of shocking white hair back off his face and reached his chin to the ceiling. With eyes closed, he placed his fingertips on his hard bone cheeks and slowly brailled through the valleys and canyons of his stubble. Robert felt his grandfather's body growing larger in the steam. The huge muscular thighs, the hard stomach, the long hairy legs, and the brown spots covering the tight elastic vastness of his grandfather's skin like war medals.

Robert's grandfather dipped his horsehair brush into the water, stirred it in the bowl of foam, and lathered the right side of his face. He draped a linen cloth over his left shoulder. Pulling the skin from his right ear towards his chin with his left hand, he began to scrape the straight razor down his face towards his jawline. After each careful scrape he wiped the foam onto the linen cloth. The transformation had begun. Rochester was waiting.

Robert could hear the deep sigh breathing from the kitchen. He wanted to let go of the toilet paper. He thought he could feel slippery eels oozing down his back ready to slide into the bathtub.

Will Coutts was obsessed with good health. Several years back he discovered his hair was thinning. That was when he began to participate in a cure for the balding little circle on top of his old-man head. This ritual also involved his grandson. Every Sunday afternoon.

Robert would hold the slimy blood-soaked tin, red gobs of shapeless liver, arm stretched toward his gagging grandfather. Cannibals and hearts of buffalo, lifted from the tin, sliding down like raw egg, blood dribbling in the corner of Will Coutts' mouth as he accepted the wide-throat sacrifice, the medicine man's cure for falling hair. Down it would go — slippery easy like an eel.

Robert was sure he could hear the red gobs of raw liver growing in the tin on the side of the bathtub, but remembered it wasn't Sunday. Today was Monday, he reassured himself. It was Monday.

His grandfather's hair started to grow back at the same time as a marvellous new beard began to grow from the bottom of his chin, joining the hair on his chest. Will Coutts was a healthy man.

Noises of pots and pans moving about began from the other room. The breathing became faster and heavier and loud footsteps pounded on the linoleum kitchen floor. The old man started to scrape away the stubble on the left side of his face.

Robert knew he'd never be as healthy as his grandfather. He figured he'd probably be bald and crippled over with polio by the time he was thirty. And he knew it was his own fault. His grandfather had tried to give him a healthy start to life.

Every morning Robert was bounced cold-turkey awake by squeaky springs and a flip-flopping mattress. When he snapped open his eyes he'd once again see his grandfather's hairy legs pedalling high in the air as he began his morning exercises. Robert wondered how he survived the earthquake and wasn't squashed flat when he was a baby.

Every morning it was the same routine. When he finished his exercises on the bed, Will Coutts would stand and stretch his colossal arms in homage to the cracked plastered ceiling, groaning like the trains moving in for repairs down at the roundhouse. Then he would run, double time, up and down, on the spot, knees to hands, counting loudly, slap slap, to one hundred and fifty. Robert would watch him take his overalls, the same ones he wore everyday, out of the wardrobe. After he put them on he'd pick up the big pot and throw his nighttime piss out the window. Now the day could really get going.

Will would go into the kitchen and start the porridge cooking on the stove. He'd return to his grandson with a cardboard box. Robert would sit up. From jars and bottles came spoons full of magic substances guaranteeing years of good health and lush hair. Black thick molasses, gobbed and clinging for dear life onto the spoon, coming closer and closer to Robert's mouth. Swallowing it — awake! Cod liver oil — awake! Wheat germ — awake! Brewer's yeast, powdered garlic, lecithin — awake, awake, awake! Then the parade of little ladybug pills and brown tablets. Vitamins A and B and C and D. Calcium and potassium and magnesium and zinc. Niacin and Pantothenic Acid. On and on and finished off with a large bowl of porridge, eaten lump by nourishing lump. Then Robert was allowed to get out of bed, stepping with bare feet onto the cold Saskatchewan floor. Now could a grandfather try harder than that?

Robert found out pretty early on that it was possible to trick a blind man. He still had to swallow the thick gobby stuff but the vitamins and pills found their way into a hole in the plaster. Year after year. When the capsules became permanent insulation against the long draughty winters and rose to the top of the hole, the crime was uncovered. Will Coutts still had an acute sense of smell and the evidence was absolute.

Added years to his life — down the drain! Protection from disease — wasted! Brain power — squandered! Robert's shame was met with stony silence and an unusual home improvement act as the plaster hit the hole. Robert would have preferred the shit to hit the fan. He learned about the power of his grandfather's silence. Yes, he would surely be bald and crippled over with polio by the time he was thirty.

Robert hoped he would never disappoint his grandfather again. He held on even more tightly to the roll of toilet paper as Will Coutts began the final campaign in his conquest against total blindness. He gently pulled up his nose with his left hand and with the certainty of a surgeon began a series of miniature downward slices towards his upper lip. The steam was lifting. The time was getting close.

A scream came from the kitchen — a high screeching wail as the kettle boiled over on the stove. The razor sliced down into Will Coutts' lip. "Goddamn you woman," he bellowed.

Goddamn yourself, thought Flo, pouring the water into her teapot. Goddamn you yourself.

Robert started whipping the toilet paper off the roll. No, it's not time — it's not time, he told himself. His grandfather thrashed down the razor and plunged his face into the sink. Robert started rolling up the loose toilet paper, careful not to rip a square, as his grandfather drenched the second face cloth, twisted the water out, slapped it on his face, and leaned his head once more against the back of the chair.

I'll have my cup of tea, thought Flo. I won't be a prisoner in my own house. The old man'll get dinner on the twelve o'clock. I'll make some soup and me and Robert can sit down when he gets back from the station. He can catch the train to bloody hell for all I care.

Flo sat down at the kitchen table and stewed. She wondered if he'd actually get all the way to Rochester — or if he'd get off in Saskatoon. Well either way was fine with her. At least he'd be out of the house. She was going to carry on. Mrs. Potts and Mrs. Jenkins could come over at two and she'd read them their tea leaves. Mrs. Jenkins could bring her Pekinese this time. The dog had made it through eighteen Saskatchewan winters. She'd stop over and tell her when the old man gets out of her hair.

Or maybe she'd read the cards. Flo hadn't the heart to show Mrs. Potts the ace of spades when it reared its ugly head the last time. It wasn't about any of her husbands. They were all dead thank God. It was about the niece she kept in her basement with a washing machine. The cards kept spelling out disaster for the poor girl. Flo didn't know how Gladys was going to manage the laundry business if something happened to Edna. She'd probably have to work harder at getting another husband.

Flo looked at the cardboard boxes on the kitchen floor. At least if he gets his eye fixed, she thought, I could throw out all that damn lotion and eye-drop shit. She bit harder into the side of her mouth. I hope to God he does it.

Will Coutts leaned towards the sink and let the face cloth drop off. Then he took a clean white towel and once again sat back against the chair with the towel falling onto his uplifted face. With the palms of his hands he patted the moisture into the flannel like the gentle expert coaxing of a baby's burp. He stopped.

Robert nervously fingered the end of the toilet paper. He waited. Will Coutts stayed seated and swivelled towards Robert. He raised his body in the chair, stiff like the tomb mummy in Saturday afternoon serials down at the movie theatre. The bandaged skull . . . what was there? . . . what was there?

Robert was ready. His grandfather pulled at the bottom of the towel and unveiled the naked terrain of his conquered face, glistening in its magnificence. Robert sat there, tense and concentrated, the pale blue jellyfish floating wide beneath the deep shadow river of the eye . . . waiting for it . . . waiting.

One by one, tiny little blood beads popped out from all over Will Coutts' face and started their migratory journey down to his neck. Robert revved into action.

Rip, lick, paste. Rip, lick, paste. Faster, faster! Rip, lick, paste. Rip, lick, paste. The blood beads were coming in battalions.

Not for a moment did Robert lose his concentration. He could handle anything. He worked like the dickens. On and on until the task was done.

And when he was absolutely certain the well was dried up, he sat back on the bathtub and surveyed his victory. He counted seventeen blood-gobbed shrivelled little pieces of toilet paper decorating his grandfather's chin, cheeks, forehead and nose.

Step one had gone without a hitch. Step two would be pulling them off.

Will Coutts stood up tentatively, careful not to let any of Robert's work fall off his face. He left the instruments and remnants of his Monday morning massacre strewn all over the bathroom. Robert followed him as he walked through the kitchen and into his bedroom at the back of the house. Robert glimpsed his granny, tight-lipped and staring into her tea.

Will sat down on the edge of the bed and started putting on his boots. Robert helped him. As he finished lacing, Robert looked over and saw his grandmother standing on the kitchen side of the doorway, peering in at her husband as if she were trying to solve some great puzzle. It made the boy feel nervous all over again.

After his grandfather put on a starched white shirt and notched up the top of his overalls, he lay his huge body, boots and all, down on the bed. He closed his eyes and crossed his arms over his chest. Robert slipped up on the bed onto his knees and looked down at his grandfather's face. He wondered if this was what a corpse looked like.

When Robert began the painstaking task of tugging off the seventeen little bloodsuckers, he looked over again at his grandmother. She was now standing with her arms stretched against the frame in the doorway, looking as if she were holding up the inside of the house, just like the arms of the caragana bushes looked as if they were holding up the outside. He hoped to goodness she wasn't going to take one more step into enemy territory.

Robert picked and peeled, picked and peeled, careful not to leave any paper bits or start the blood flowing again. He felt the shadow at the door and heard his grandfather breathe more quickly as his grandmother sighed more deeply. It was a stand-off.

I wish I had a TV, thought Robert. Pick and peel. Pick and peel.

The muscles of Will Coutts' face were as disciplined as a ventriloquist's. He threw his voice out of his body and over towards the door. "Goddamn you woman, get out of my room."

She threw her voice back in. "I'm not in your goddamn room you old bugger. I'm at the door and I'm not budgin'." And she didn't.

Pick and peel. Pick and peel.

During the past summer, the modern world had snuck over from the Rocky Mountains and settled in Saskatchewan. A couple of old-timers with no kids had purchased the first Biggar television set. They were operating it down at the bottom of Second Avenue. The machine was placed in such a way that if you stood by the fence outside their yard it was possible to see the reflection catching in the window. You couldn't see the picture but you knew something was moving and it was great. A sign went up in their front yard late in the summer. PLEASE DON'T LEAN ON THE FENCE. Crowds of drooling children used to start gathering at around seven-thirty every evening. When the fence tumbled over, Melanie Perkins' skirt went flying right over her head. "Television is great," said Jimmy Higgins' older brother Gary.

Ron Hayes and Jane Leikam's parents both bought television sets for their kids in the fall. Robert knew there was no hope in hell that his grandparents would ever get a TV.

When he'd finished picking his way through his grandfather's face, Robert glanced over to see his granny still holding her ground. She hadn't moved. Robert saddled over to the window sill at the edge of the bed not knowing where to look. Behind him was his grandfather's backyard. He couldn't look out there. Robert hated the secret ice-bumpy shapes that always thawed out and tried to get him . . . rusty tin cans, spiked two-by-fours, greased axles, tin slabs, wound wire, coils, tires, frozen rat shit, old piss and rhubarb. In the springtime, even the robins stayed out of the backyard. Robert decided just to close his eyes.

He heard his grandfather get off the bed, put on his parka and pick up his suitcase. He heard him walk over to the door. He didn't hear his grandmother budge.

In the blackness of his eyes he saw the chicken body running through the house like a crazy bird looking for its chicken head.

"Goddamn you woman, get out of my way!"

Still nobody moved.

Robert could hear his heartbeat pounding. He felt as if he were at the Saturday afternoon movies just when the hero gets sucked into the foaming quicksand and the action stops and the screen flashes "WILL THE CAPTAIN BE RESCUED? . . . COME BACK NEXT WEEK FOR THE EXCITING CONCLUSION OF CAPTAIN INCREDIBLE AND THE ALLI-GATOR PIT!"

Robert couldn't stand it any more. He banged open his eyes. There they were. His grandparents. Standing a foot away from each other. Nose to nose.

Nobody budged.

Just as he decided that it might be easier to look over his shoulder and into the backyard, his grandmother spoke.

"Good luck, Will," she said, and went back to her tea at the table.

The Dow Jones Average

Flo Coutts stood over the stove cooking the midday meal. Every day at quarter to twelve, blind old Will Coutts pushed his way up Second Avenue, his wheelbarrow guiding him through the town like a Seeing Eye dog. He'd dump out the scrap pieces of useful junk he collected from the property he owned down on Main Street into his backyard. Although he didn't stand a chance of finding any of it again, all items were diligently catalogued in his mind. He then entered his house through the front door, not saying a word to his wife, and straight into the bathroom to wash his feet.

When his three daughters lived at home they had the task of bringing a warm basin of water from the coal-burning stove and washing his feet for him. After they headed out for the coast, Will was left to service his own feet. Flo flatly refused. All seven children got out of the house as soon as they could. Flo imagined them sitting in a row on a pier, toes dangling in the Pacific, soaking away the sins of the parents and the stench of hard living.

After his feet were clean, Will would go into his bedroom at the back of the house and turn on the radio to listen to the stock market report, which came on before the twelve o'clock news. Rumour about town was the old bugger had a fortune tied up in stocks and bonds, and when he died Flo and the children would be left a bundle. And the rumour was true.

Meanwhile they lived in an old slum of a house like people on social assistance and Will was so healthy he'd probably outlive them all. Will Coutts didn't believe in spending money. Money was too important.

When the town whistle went off at twelve o'clock, Flo would hang her great shaking body out the front door and yell for her grandson. ROOOOOBERT! Robert's mother left her newborn baby with her parents five years ago. It was meant to be temporary while she created a better life for herself and her son in Vancouver. She came back once a year in late summer and bought her mother a new piece of furniture or a coat.

Robert spent the days with his grandmother in the front part of the small house and evenings with his grandfather, sharing his bedroom at the back. The hard part was lunch and supper when he had to spend time with the two of them together.

Flo flipped the fish over in the fry pan and stirred the beans.

As Will lay on his back listening to the bad news on the stock market report, his grandson knelt above him on the bed. The boy squeezed the little rubber bulb, dipping it into the brown medicine bottle a doctor from Saskatoon gave his grandfather for the one eye that still saw shadows. Robert peered down into the wide-open battlefield of the cataract eye. He sucked the green liquid up into the rubber space station and swung the deadly doomsday machine out over the target. Eye naked to the ceiling, Robert aimed at the pale blue saucer floating behind the drifting camouflage . . . BOMBS

AWAY . . . SPLASH . . . BULLS EYE! Driblets of guck slimed out and onto his grandfather's cheek. Unflinching, Will Coutts listened and fumed, as the announcer confirmed, one after the other, the month-long dip in the value of his investments.

Will Coutts sat at the kitchen table and scowled. Flo asked him if he didn't like the fish.

"I don't give a damn about the goddamn fish," he replied.

Robert made the mistake of saying that the Dow Jones average was sickening.

"It's weak — not sickening," barked his grandfather.

"It'll all turn out just fine in the end whatever it is," comforted Flo. "Things do. Just look at World War Two or that Finlayson boy who got out of jail and got that job sellin' encyclopaedias. And what about Lilly Cook's granddaughter? She's growing at such a rate they thought the little darlin' had cancer of the thyroid. But no, that baby's gonna be just fine they said. She'll be as big as a house and that's the end of it. Don't worry about Dow Jones and eat your fish."

"God you're a stupid old woman Flo. Things don't just turn out fine. How the hell do you think I get the money to put food on your table? If the Dow Jones average keeps falling we'll be in the poorhouse by June."

"We live like we're in the poorhouse now you old bugger. I don't see what difference it would make."

Robert thought about the macaroni and white bread they were probably eating over at Billy Palmer's and wished he didn't have to eat this stupid healthy stuff his granny bought from the Co-op.

"If you have your way, you'll put us in the poorhouse yet Flo. You know as much about money as you do about thyroids. You listen so much to that Gladys Potts your brain's shrivelled to the size of a peanut. Dow Jones and Lilly Cook!

Christ, you're such an expert about Dow Jones and finance you might as well trot up to the university in Saskatoon and ask for your Bachelor of Commerce degree."

"I don't have to put us in the poorhouse because we're already there, you old skinflint. You got money coming out of your goddamn you-know-what and you expect me to bring home the groceries and make a life year after year in this run-down slum of a dump on that measly little allowance you give me week after week. Heaven forbid we end up in the poor-house Will. Maybe we'll just have to pack our bags and move into some of that property downtown and live there hey. You own half of Main Street you old slum-landlord miser so don't give me no more shit about going to the poorhouse!"

Robert figured his grandmother had gone a bit too far when she called him a landlord and thought harder about the white bread and cornflakes Billy got to have every morning for breakfast instead of porridge and molasses.

Will hadn't heard a word his wife was saying. He was thinking about the time in Calgary after he'd married her. She was sixteen and kept running home to her sisters saying she didn't want to be married to an old man. He tried to make her feel better so he went out and bought her a whole house load of new furniture from Eatons. When he came home the next day, she'd thrown every piece of it onto the front yard. So to hell with that, he'd thought. Even in Biggar, whenever she got something half decent she'd give it away. If someone liked something, she'd hand the damn thing over. Came home one day when his good eye was still working to see the Christly Presbyterian Minister and that Mrs. Potts bitch standing in the kitchen. Flo was about to give the goddamn kitchen cupboard to the church. The church for Christ Sake! Why not to the bingo parlour or the legion if she has to give it to someone? Flo'd never been in a church in her life. Will figured when the old woman kicks the bucket, he'd probably have to hold the funeral service in the backyard.

So for thirty-five years Will Coutts took care of the money. At the beginning of every week, Flo was given a small household allowance for groceries and essentials. If she needed anything extra, she had to ask him for it. All bills were accounted for at the end of the week.

Flo sat there looking at her fish. It was the first conversation they'd had in ages and she wondered why he shut up just when she was telling him off. She chewed the left side of her lip with particular vigour. Finally she couldn't stand the silence any longer.

"And when was the last time I bought something for myself hey? Answer me that you old bugger. I'll move to the poorhouse with you Will, but I won't go there looking like a tramp."

Robert got really nervous. He started to laugh.

"You know what Robert. Why don't I just give your grandmother a million dollars right now? Why don't I just hand it over. She can go downtown this afternoon and buy herself a whole new fandangled wardrobe. And maybe a hundred and fifty new hats to wear for tea down at the poorhouse!"

Robert didn't want to go to the poorhouse. He wanted to go to Billy's.

"I wouldn't take a million dollars from you if you begged me on your hands and knees."

"Well I wouldn't give you a million dollars because if I gave you a million dollars you'd give the whole damn million away!"

Flo stood up. "You know what you are Will Coutts. You're just a THREE HUNDRED POUND . . . TUB OF LARD!"

Will stood up. "And you know what you are Flo. You're just a FIVE HUNDRED POUND TUB OF SHIT!"

And he walked into his bedroom.

Flo sat back down and scraped dried-up food off the plastic tablecloth with her fingernail. Robert waited. He wanted to go play with Billy but figured he should wait.

When Will Coutts walked out the front door, Flo went to the kitchen counter and gobbed a tablespoon of butter into her mouth. She told her grandson to put on his coat. They were going downtown.

Robert and his grandmother stood in front of Woolworths. They didn't go in. They just stood there looking through the window. Looking at hats.

Flo saw her great tub of lard body staring back at her from the glass. She thought about her older sisters in Alberta and their comfortable lives. Anne with her gin and tonics; Millie with her goddamn trip to Hawaii once a year — painting ALOHA on her roof so all the people flying overhead would know that she too was part of the privileged tourist class.

And here was Flo stuck in the piss-pot of the earth. Fat and stupid. She'd been prettier and more fun than the pair of them put together. "Marry the old man," they said. "He has money — you'll never have to worry."

Robert was wishing they could go stand in front of the pool hall instead of this stupid department store when his granny suddenly pulled him away and told him they were going home to cut his hair.

The next morning Flo stayed in her room. Robert wondered why she was in there for so long. He could smell the powder-puff stuff she put on her face. He wanted to go in to find out, but the last time he went into his grandmother's room he saw her big bum and she got very mad at him and told him never to come into her room again without knocking.

Robert didn't feel like knocking that morning. He just felt like going in. So he waited for her instead. He wondered about those stupid itchy pants his grandmother had ironed after she had stuck the bowl on his head to cut his hair.

The moment his grandfather left for his wheelbarrow, his grandmother, already wearing her coat, boomed out of the bedroom. "Let's put on your good pants," she commanded, lipstick all over her lips and powder-puff stuff puff-puffing through the living room.

Oh no, not the pants, he thought.

Flo had just counted the twenty-three dollars she'd been saving in her underwear drawer. Every Saturday night she played bingo down at the legion and every Saturday night she won. She usually won twice. The prizes were laid out on a table in the centre of the room. Instead of choosing the glass tumblers or jigsaw puzzles, or even the enormous bag of chocolate-covered raisins, regular as clockwork she picked a bag of flour on her first win and a bag of sugar on her second. At the end of the week she included them in the expense list demanded by Will and stashed the loot in with her underwear. Who says I don't know nothin' about finance, she thought to herself.

Robert sat on a chair and negotiated his feet through the leg holes, trying not to let any of the itchy material touch his skin. He was about to take a rest when his granny grabbed the waistband and yanked it up to his armpits, jerking him right off the chair. She buckled his belt, tossed him his coat, and off they went to Lilly Cook's.

Flo asked Lilly to take some lunch in for the old man at twelve and to tell him she and Robert would be home for supper. Robert had to stand in all his itchiness and tell Lilly's little daughter that her enormous baby was just as cute as anything.

Robert heard the wailing of the steam engine coming in from the west. They were standing on the station platform with all the others who came to watch the trains pull in and out of Biggar. It was rumbling towards them when Flo gave him the news — they were going to Saskatoon for the day. They weren't going to just stand there with all the poor onlookers waiting for the locomotive to pull out so they could go home to their ironing and cooking and Dow Jones Average lives. No! They were actually going to step on the platform to climb aboard. They were going to Saskatoon and life was great!

"AAAALL ABOARD"

The conductor walked up the aisle asking for tickets. When he came to Robert's granny, he gave her a big wink, tipped his hat, and walked on by. Robert's granny had a pass. Before his grandpa started going blind, he'd worked as a linesman on the railroad, so his granny got to travel for free.

Robert leaned into the comfort of his grandmother's flesh, looking out at the vastness of the passing world and knowing that his grandfather must be right. The universe goes on forever.

He knew sitting in the train with his grandmother was much better than sitting under the sink in the kitchen. He used to sit against the wall that was close to the sink, but one day Mrs. Potts told him God was everywhere. So as he was sitting with his back against the wall, close to the sink, he thought to himself, all right then, if God is everywhere, I'm going to see this God. He looked to the right — nothing. To the left — nothing. Then quickly to the right — and to the left — and straight up — and down. Nothing. Nothing. And then he saw little bits of dust catching the light as they floated through the kitchen air and he thought, maybe that's him? Maybe those are bits of God? I can see it everywhere. Just then a big pile of plaster fell off the ceiling and landed on his head. So he moved over and from then on sat under the sink.

Flo felt the same empty sadness as when she first looked out onto that Godforsaken prairie earth. She thought about arriving in Biggar thirty-five years ago with an ancient husband who didn't utter a word during the entire trip from Calgary. She remembered the smells of being a nineteen-year-old mother and the eyes of her newborn baby looking up at her. Please take me home to the lush wet kindness of Yorkshire, they'd say. I don't want to grow up here. There must be some mistake.

She always hated the chug-chug chugging of the train. It felt like it was shaking away her past.

Where was her mother? And that darling boy — the brother who left to be a singer in New York City when they got off the boat in Montreal; the brother who abandoned her to the New World greed of her older sisters when they got on the train to Calgary? And where was beautiful young Flo — the sweetheart who made heads spin faster than both her sisters put together; who could charm every man on board from Quebec to Alberta? Where was she?

Will and his wife moved to Biggar after his partner from Edmonton cheated Will out of everything in their lumber business. They moved to a speck on the map because the speck on the map was a town with a future. It was destined to become the New York City of Western Canada. Two railway companies, the Grand Trunk Pacific and the Canadian Pacific, chose to cross their tracks through a town plunked in the middle of one of the fastest growing provinces in Canada. Unity, Wilkie, Kindersley, North Battleford, Rosetown, Perdue, Leipzig, Springwater — BIGGAR! Now who could deny the BOOM TOWN RING of that?

Flo spent thirty-five years looking into babies' eyes, vowing she would not be defeated by a speck on the map or by Will Coutts. She worked like hell all day, but there wasn't an evening she didn't step out on the town. Every night at six she put on a clean dress and it was out the door — even in later years if it was just to listen to the new clean linoleum squeaking at Gladys Potts'. It was a good thing she had three daughters to take care of the younger ones. No wonder they got out of town so fast.

Down at the Majestic Theatre, in the days when vaudeville still toured the West, she met Bob Clappet.

As the train forever rolled on into the universe, Robert looked up at his grandmother. She was chewing the left side of her lip with a vengeance. It reminded him of how she looked sometimes in the mornings, whole-wheat flour and beads of sweat sticking to her face as she baked a rhubarb pie, gobbing tablespoons of butter into her mouth and singing sad songs to him under the sink. Sometimes the sweat and flour would clump together with her tears.

On mornings when his granny was feeling particularly miserable, she made up her own words and sang along to the tunes on the radio. There were times when the songs were so depressing, Robert couldn't help sobbing along with her.

*Frankie and Johnny were lovers — but Johnny's gone
far far away
I'm standin' here bakin' a pie dear — hopin' you'll
come back some day
Oh I need my man — I need him bad
The old kitchen cupboards are empty — the damp
and the cold's comin' through
Little Willy he died in a crib death — along with your
sweet baby Sue
Oh I'm baking a pie — trying hard not to cry
I listen so long for your footsteps — the baby she's
cryin' away
Little Bobby's gone off to the war dear — they turned
off the heat yesterday
Oh I need a man — I need him bad
Are you comin' round the corner, my Johnny? — do I
hear ya walkin' home down the street?
Are ya bringing some groceries my darlin'? — 'cause
we really need something to eat
Oh I'm baking a pie — trying hard not to cry
I forgive you my darling for hurtin' — I forgive you
my sweet husband dear
Oh my love burns so sweet for your footsteps — but my
heart pounds so loud with such fear
Oh I need my man — and I need him oh sooo
baaaad
Oh yeah . . . Oh yeah . . . Oh yeah . . .*

On and on — the tears gushing over his granny's chubby
cheeks, spewing flour and sweat and traces of butter into a
little puddle of despair on the floor in front of Robert's sink.

Finally the great steam engine came to a screeching halt
in the city of Saskatoon. Right on time. An hour out of Biggar.

The conductor put down the landing box and held out his hand as Flo stepped off the train. Mrs. Coutts and her grandson walked the expansive platform past porters and expensive luggage and onto the corridor that took them under the tracks and up into the station. Flo and her grandson proceeded at a fairly brisk gait through the waiting room and into the heart of Saskatoon.

The small boy looked up at the towering city. He thought about his Superman comics and the Man of Steel flying above the skyscrapers. He kept his eyes peeled for bad guys and loved the oil-slick smell of the fancy cars.

Flo held tightly onto Robert's hand and headed toward her destination. She knew exactly where she was going. She marched up to the front of a tall brick building and pushed at the glass door. It whipped forward, spun a circle, and before Robert knew it he'd been yanked in and spat out on the other side. It was the biggest store he'd ever seen.

Flo walked to the far back corner of the store and sat down in a chair in front of a mirror. She told Robert to sit on the bench behind her.

The same clerk who served her the last time she was in the store noticed her immediately. Flo watched him slither over in the same tight blue suit, his greasy hair circling his bald spot. He's the sort of person who can't help squeaking, she thought.

"Well, if it isn't the lovely lady from North Battleford," squeaked the salesman.

"I'm from Biggar and I ain't no lady," replied Mrs. Coutts.

The man brought her three hats. A pale green hat which Flo quite liked except for the purple trim. A larger brown hat with two rooster feathers Flo could swear were crowing sideways towards the lingerie department. And a little black banana hat that looked like a half moon.

She put one hat on after the other. And then she did it again. She looked at them from the right side and then from the left. She asked the salesman what he thought. He said at different times that each one was most certainly his favourite. Then she lined them all up in a row and stepped way back into the cosmetic department to look at them from a distance. When she walked back, she handed over a ten-dollar bill and picked up the little black moon.

Mrs. Coutts, her grandson and a brand-new Eaton's shopping bag whirled their way through the swinging door and were deposited back onto the street.

Dragging her grandson, Flo walked with great deliberation back to the train station. She saw the same conductor who'd been on the incoming train standing out front and asked him when the next train left from Biggar. He told her the next train left Biggar in about five minutes — arriving in Saskatoon in just over an hour, at about one-thirty.

She asked the conductor to keep an eye on her grandson and went inside to make a telephone call.

When she came back, Flo bought Robert some Crackerjacks and made him sit on a bench in the station lobby. She told him to wait there while she visited the ladies' room. Robert watched an old man out the window drinking from a brown paper bag and seven gangsters hanging around the newsstand chewing gum. He wondered how his grandfather was gonna make out with the brown medicine bottle and hoped he'd hit the bull's eye.

Flo came out of the ladies' room with fresh lipstick, rouge on her cheeks, and a black half moon perched like a cheeky little smile on the side of her head. Robert could smell perfume.

They walked through the corridor, under the tracks, and up onto the platform on the other side. Flo went to the far end to the lost luggage room and asked if she and her grandson could sit there for a while. Robert expected his granny to say she had a pass, but they must have known because they let her.

Robert sat on a trunk while his granny stood looking out the door. He couldn't figure out what they were doing. Maybe they were hiding? Maybe they were going to surprise someone who got off the train from Biggar?

At one-thirty, Flo was primed. She licked down the last few strands of loose hair and took one final suck on her teeth. The train rolled in. She held Robert's hand tightly, and as soon as the passengers started disembarking, they joined the stream of people heading for the corridor that took them under the tracks and into the station lobby.

Robert still couldn't figure out what was going on. They were getting off the train from Biggar and walking into Saskatoon all over again. Robert thought that maybe his granny was going back for the hat with the rooster feathers.

"Don't say nothin' about the hat," Flo said out of the side of her mouth.

Robert's grandmother stopped. A man was smiling and walking towards her. A man. A man with a patch.

Flo knew she couldn't have met Bob Clappet the way she looked when she got off the train that morning. So she phoned him, pretending she was calling from Biggar. Told him she was coming in for a little outing with her grandson. Then she bought a hat.

Robert didn't feel the same tightness on his hand. His grandmother seemed to be flying away in her moon hat.

The man with the eye patch came over and said, "My God Flo, you look like a million bucks. Biggar's startin' to suit ya!" and then he laughed a fat laugh.

Bob Clappet turned and bent down so close Robert knew he could have touched his patch if he wanted to. But he didn't because he thought it might be holding in a glass eye.

"Hiya, Robert, you look like a million bucks too — great pants!" And he laughed again.

The man smelled clean — really clean — cleaner than his grandfather's shaving bowl. Robert didn't want to look into his one good eye because he thought he might go permanently cross-eyed. The man gave Robert an airplane made out of balsam wood. Robert could feel the hot itchy scratching of his woollen trousers.

Mr. Clappet and Mrs. Coutts walked slowly down the platform promenade, under the tracks, and proceeded through the lobby into the City of Sin.

Robert noticed the old man by the window was still drinking his pop out of a paper bag. He let go of his granny's hand because it felt mushy and he didn't let the patch guy grab his other hand because it probably played catch with his glass eye. If he even had a glass eye! Maybe it was just a hole. It would be easy to drop stuff in though, thought Robert. He walked behind them noticing that the patch guy's bum was as big as his granny's.

They went into a restaurant. Robert had a chocolate milkshake and french fries and all three of them sat on orange stools. When Robert's granny and the patch guy laughed, their bodies shook together like jello trucks and their bums flapped over the seats.

Robert's granny seemed to forget all about him and didn't even ask for a slurp of his milkshake, so he decided not to listen to anything they were talking about. He just spun round and round on his stool. The cushions were puffed up hard and glossy. He felt like he was twirling high on the greasy circle of the hat-man's bald spot, or on top of the patch guy's large frozen eyeball.

Mr. Clappet asked Flo how life was with the old man.

Robert kept on twirling — his granny was laughing too loud.

Bob Clappet lived in Saskatoon with his wife Ethel. He'd known Flo for thirty years — ever since he first performed at the Majestic Theatre. She'd sit in the second row with two, sometimes three babies, laughing louder than anybody else. Every couple of years when he came back through town, he'd bring her magazines and perfume. Even when vaudeville became less popular and he had to marry Ethel, who owned a boarding house in Saskatoon, he always found a way to rent that little room on top of the beer parlour at the hotel in Biggar. Next to the bootlegger down on Avenue C, Flo was the person who made him laugh harder than anyone.

Robert kept on twirling and wondered why his grandfather didn't get a patch.

Flo Coutts had been discreet. She didn't see him often, but when she did she had a hell of a time. Even though she only saw Bob once every couple of years, he never stopped making her feel loved.

He was the only one besides her brother who made her feel like the "darling one"— her brother who left her to go to New York to be a singer . . . her darling brother who died a drunkard before he was thirty.

Bob was a singer too — and a drunk — but he had too much loving in his belly to die on anyone. He was a warm fat pillow of a man and reminded her of the wet countryside of Yorkshire, where she'd lived with her parents until her goddamn sisters made her travel to the goddamn Wild West in the goddamn New World. Bob was the only Wild West she'd ever run into and although she didn't see him often, and even forgot about him for years on end, she knew when it was time. And it was time.

Robert twirled so hard he spun off the stool, a stream of chocolate spraying out of his mouth — puking its way to the back of the restaurant where a little chewed up french fry landed plop in the middle of a woman's chicken salad sandwich.

Mr. Clappet paid the woman's bill and apologized for laughing so hard. Flo told Robert that they'd better hurry if they were going to make it to the station for the three-thirty and get home in time to make supper for his grandpa.

Standing on the train platform, Bob adjusted the black half-moon so it sat even further back on Flo's head and whispered in her ear.

"I"m gonna be doing some business in that little town of yours tomorrow, Flo. There's a little song I want to sing above the beer parlour tomorrow afternoon."

"Nice to meet ya Robert. Try not ta throw up over anyone's chicken sandwich on the train. Great pants!"

The first thing Flo did when she got on board was go into the washroom to take off her hat. She sat with her grandson and chewed her lip for a while thinking about what she was going to make for supper. She tried not to worry about how often they changed the sheets above the beer parlour. Then she turned to Robert.

"Just put your head on my tummy sweetheart. Close your eyes and listen to the ocean. We'll be home soon."

Robert rested his head on his granny's great rumbling stomach and closed his eyes.

"And don't say nothin' to your grandpa about the hat okay. It'll just make him . . . you know. He's got enough to worry about with that Dow Jones fellah. And I wouldn't mention anything about . . . you know. You can tell him about the milkshake. He's sort of mad with your granny at the moment so let's just tell him about the milkshake. We don't want him stewin' about the poorhouse."

Robert rested into the mammoth warmth of his grandmother's body and listened to the far distant oceans and felt the spray. Rocking back and forth with the rhythm of the train, his head sunk deep into the wet octopus seas of his grandmother's stomach and he heard the great giant whales flip-flopping through the misty cloudbanks of his grandfather's eye.

On and on, forever into the universe, singing . . .
Robert and his granny were lovers — and they had a
very fine day
Someone dropped their eye ball down an outhouse —
and it floated somewhere down far away
Oh I need Superman — and I like to fish
Oh yeah . . . Oh yeah . . . Oh yeah . . .
And on and on as the train and his granny rocked him further and further into a deep sleep.

When Robert got home the first thing he did was scrape off the woollen trousers. It was quarter to five but maybe he could get in some playing. Anyway he wanted to give that stupid balsam wood airplane to Billy Palmer.

He ran over to the Palmer's but nobody answered the door. He wondered what they were having for supper with their white bread. Then he took the balsam airplane thing and busted it in two. He left it for Billy on his front step.

Robert looked down the street and saw his grandfather's wheelbarrow pushing its way home. He ran all the way down to the bottom of Second Avenue.

Robert and his grandfather stood there on the street of the small prairie town.

"So Grandpa. How was the Dow Jones Average today?"

Waiting for Meadowlarks

Part One

L ouise wondered whether her son Robert was still asleep.
She'd woken up early in the ridiculous little room her
father made by dividing up part of the veranda. If she reached
above her head, she could have tapped on the window to her
mother's bedroom.

At least I'm on the outside, she sighed. Imagine looking
through your bedroom window out onto another bedroom.
Just like one of those paintings by what's his name. Looking
out onto another. And another. No way out. Sleeping on a
lumpy old mattress night after night, hoping for something
better. Surely she must still hope for something better.

I wish she'd let me buy her a new bed.

Could anything be more ridiculous than sleeping outside
your mother's window, she wondered? I suppose if this was
a little family hotel in Europe somewhere my mother could
open the window and pass me French pastries and coffee for
breakfast. Maybe she should start some kind of restaurant
trade right here in Biggar — all the guys from the Wheat Pool
sitting on the veranda drinking margaritas and spreading pâté
on a French loaf. I wonder if she knows what pâté is? I know

she doesn't know what a French pastry is. Christ, sometimes I wonder if she even knows what the Wheat Pool is.

I really should buy her a new bed.

Louise thought about her brothers and sisters, and how they ever fit into this pathetic excuse for a house. And poor Peter, the last in a long line of seven, banished to the cold veranda with a horse blanket and a marconi set. At least he was always on the outside, she thought.

She could hear her mother's substantial body snoring and turning on the bed. How long had it been since her father had slept with her? Sleep hell, how long since he'd even said something nice to her. She couldn't remember when her parents had shared a room. It seemed her father had been born in the back of the house. Born to be a miserable old bugger counting his money and eating health food junk to make sure he'd never die. Heaven forbid if he died — somebody might spend his money.

When they were growing up, none of her brothers or sisters could imagine their parents ever having sex. I suppose that's the same with all children, she thought. Problem is I still can't imagine it. And I don't want to. I wish they'd get up.

Maybe I can get Robert out of bed before my father wakes? I need to get him out of the house where we can talk. I can't talk to him in front of them — and not in this house. God I hate this house — I don't know where my brain was.

Why am I being so ungrateful? she asked herself. They've done their best for crying out loud. Who else has parents who would have done what they did? Just thank them and suffer the consequences. It's time. I feel certain of that this morning. I am his mother.

Every year in late August, Louise arrived from Vancouver to visit her son. She'd left him with her parents when he was a baby and gone to the coast to make a better life — a life that would suit a single woman bringing up a child on her own. And every summer she arrived back in Biggar, bought a gift for her mother, and went home alone.

Louise got up. She went through to the back of the house and saw the door open to her father's bedroom. Her son was sitting on the bed trying to finish the endless line-up of vitamins, minerals and healthy supplements his grandfather insisted he swallow every morning before he was allowed to put his bare feet onto that worn-out linoleum. Before he could say so long to the wise old seer and enter the daylight of his boyhood.

God, it's amazing he hasn't caught some terrible disease sleeping with the old man in that bed, she thought. I wonder how often he lets Flo in there to clean the sheets. Jesus, I wish I could buy him a new bed too.

Louise told her son to get dressed.

After she washed and had a piece of toast, they walked down Second Avenue, past the fairgrounds and out onto the open fields.

One block and you're in the country. He's going to miss this. Maybe Les will take us to his parents' cottage in the Fraser Valley on weekends. Or we'll go to Stanley Park.

Louise held gently onto her son's hand, trying to sense what his response would be to leaving his life in Biggar. She looked at the vastness of his prairie playground and felt for signs — some signal from his hand — something to make the talk easier. She knew once he started grade one next week everything would change. It would be harder.

She remembered when she was in school and some of the boys used to stick their chests in the air and boast. "One out of every three boys who go to the Biggar High School will end up in jail — beat that Jailbird Mama!" She hated those smart-ass comments even then. Such pathetic defeatists — bragging they'd found some little degree of significance at the end of the earth.

No, he's coming home. I know what is best. I'm his mother.

They walked past the baseball field in silence. Why's he so quiet, she wondered.

Robert waited for his mother to say something. She always came in the summer and she always said something. What he really liked about his mother coming was the smell of cigarettes smoking away at the end of her red fingernail stuff. She was like a spy in a movie. They could pull out his bloody fingernails and water torture him to death before he'd say anything to the Japanese.

He wondered how long they were going to walk and remembered the last time they went down past the fairgrounds. He hoped there were no meadowlarks.

Last summer his mother got him out of bed before his grandpa woke up. She helped him dress and without saying a word they walked out the front door — like they were on a secret mission. They came to some tall grass. Then they lay down in the grass on their stomachs and they waited. And waited. His mother said they were waiting for meadowlarks. Robert didn't know what a meadowlark was. But they waited. Then they got up, his mother smoked a cigarette, and she went back to Vancouver.

The next day his granny needed some eggs. And she needed them fast. So Robert had to go to Mrs. Jenkins to borrow some of her eggs. He carried them in a little box and ran home because he knew those eggs were important. But he forgot about this bulldozer that came and ploughed away half the yard at the side of his house and ran straight into the cliff. He fell flat on his face and the box took off in the air. One by one the eggs flew out and did these slow figure eights high in the sky before pitching into the caragana bushes and letting their yoke stuff slime down the branches. Robert lay there and thought about his poor granny and how he'd broken her eggs. Then the screen door opened and out she came. "For Pete's sake, Robert, get off the ground or you're gonna get polio!"

Robert soon realized that polio was very bad and lying on the ground in Biggar was one sure way to get it. He wondered about his mother taking him to lie on the ground when they had to look for meadowlarks.

The two of them stopped by the field where stock-car races were held every Saturday afternoon and people came to drink beer. Louise wanted to sit on the ground but Robert said it'd be safer if they kept standing. Anyway, he was hoping he'd be able to go call on Danny soon.

Louise pulled out a Sweet Cap from her cigarette package and told her son they had to talk about important things.

Robert thought about the important things he had to do at Danny's and watched some dust rising in the distance. It looked like a smoke-signal puffing out of his mother's cigarette. Maybe it was another spy?

He wished Danny's mum smoked. He liked pretending she was his mum and it would be better if she smoked. Robert was glad his father was dead because he hadn't ever met him anyway and nobody had so he could tell everyone that his dad was fighting the commies. He was positive his dad had tattoos. He watched the dust getting closer and thought maybe he could see a bike.

I need to know what he's thinking, Louise said to herself. I need to know what he wants. It's only fair. It's been okay for him here — I know that. But he can be happy somewhere else — and a six-year-old boy needs to be with his mother. I'm his mother.

"Robert, how do you like living with your granny and grandpa?" she began.

What a stupid thing to say, thought Robert.

Scott spun his back wheel in a spectacular finish as he came to a screeching halt. Louise had to throw down the Sweet Cap so she could get the dust out of her eyes.

"Ya Ya Ya Ya Yaieeeeeeeeee!" howled Robert.

"Hurry up. Danny says if ya don't get over to Billy's wood-pile in forty-two split seconds flat you don't get to be the robber today. You're gonna be Korean."

Robert's mother tried to join in. "Who's your friend, Robert?"

"I'm not gonna be Korean — Billy can be Korean. Ya gotta ride me double okay?"

"Who's your friend, Robert?" repeated Louise.

"That's Scott. I gotta go. Maybe you should look for meadowlarks or something?"

"Who's that lady?" asked Scott.

"Who?" said Robert as he jumped onto Scott's bike. "Oh that's Louise." And they headed back to town.

"Yaieeeeeeeeee!"

Robert's mother stood alone on the stock-car track feeling abandoned and foolish. Why didn't he call me Mum? What's wrong with Mum, she wanted to know. "I'm not Louise," she said aloud.

And why does he have to be so goddamn happy? Why do things always have to be difficult? What am I supposed to do now? Stand here in the middle of nowhere and watch my son disappear? Stand here looking for meadowlarks?

She was alarmed at the anger she felt toward her son. All right, I'll look for meadowlarks, Robert. I'll look for a goddamn meadowlark.

Louise and Flo stood at the back of Woolworths staring at beds.

"Buy me some new towels if you gotta buy me something. I don't want a new bed."

"Mum, you deserve some comforts. Let me at least buy you a new mattress."

"Let's go visit Gerry at the bank. Come on! She always asks after ya. Tell her you'll go over tonight and see the baby."

"I'll see Gerry tomorrow. Right now I'm going to buy you a mattress."

"Are your ears plugged dear? I don't want no goddamn mattress."

"You can't keep sleeping on a worn-out mattress. It's bad for your spine. It's lumpy. You need more support."

"You're talkin' about I'm fat, Louise."

"I'm talking about taking care of you Mum because you don't take care of yourself. And you are overweight, you know. It's about time you did something about it."

"Well I thank my lucky stars you've come home to tell me how to live my life. Bein' a fat stupid old lady can sure be tough when you got no one to take care of ya. Makes me proud to have such a caring daughter. Makes my fat little heart all aglow. Why don't I treat us both to some chips and gravy and then let's go over to the Chinese Restaurant and have a couple dozen egg-rolls."

"Stop it, you're making a fool of yourself."

"Well isn't that just like me, dear."

"Mum, it's not that you're fat. You just don't take care of yourself. You're an attractive woman — "

"I'm a fat woman, Louise. They should throw me in the goddamn slough!"

"Please stop it."

Flo stormed onto the street. Louise caught up to her in front of the Five and Dime.

"It gets my goat Louise. You come here year after year and start givin' advice. As if we're not good enough for you. But we're good enough to take care of your son."

"And you think I don't know why you want me to go see Gerry so bad? So you can rub my nose in the fact that she's bringing up her kid on her own."

"That's a stupid thing to say."

"Well its true. She's staying here working for peanuts at the bank and taking care of her baby. I didn't do that."

"You didn't have to do that. You got us. I want to take care of Robert."

"And I'm taking him with me this time Mum. He's not going to stay to grow up to be some idiot thug down at the wheat pool. And I'm not staying here to end up like Gerry who'll be fat as a house sleeping alone on some lumpy old mattress when she's too tired to do anything for herself."

Flo stood bone still and looked across the street at Clarence McIntyre trying to borrow another two bucks from Harry Jessop.

"I'm sorry Mum. I didn't mean that. I have no right."

"I'm ashamed of you Louise. I'm ashamed. You've got no gratitude."

Flo walked off alone down Main Street.

Louise felt embarrassed by the shame that swept over her. She was used to guilt. Shame was uncomfortable. She felt the glare of the hot sun exposing her true self to all the disapproving eyes burning into her from Main Street. The people she'd self-righteously dismissed as idiots and thugs. The people who could see her for exactly what she was — a selfish mother who abandons her child to the care of her parents and returns once a year to criticize them; an ungrateful daughter who tries to buy off her mother with a new bed. How obvious.

She started walking home up the back alleys hoping she might catch sight of Robert playing with his friends. I need his forgiveness, she thought. I need him to love me.

She thought about Gerry and her baby. No, I'm not going to stop over to see her. I'll drop by at the bank just before I leave and apologize. She chose to have a kid and bring it up on her own. I didn't. She's a good mother. I'm not.

Do they think I wanted to leave my son here? Here in this pathetic little excuse for a town living with two people who hate each other. I was nineteen years old and my husband was dead. I didn't ask to be pregnant.

Louise could see the house in front of her and knew she had to calm down before going in.

I've got to start being more grateful, she decided. I'm the one who did it for Christ's sake. I dumped him here. And I've got to stop saying such mean things to my mum. I've got to be reasonable. Explain to her about the school thing. She'll understand. She's a mother.

Will Coutts, Flo, Louise and her son were sitting down to their midday meal. As usual, the only conversation was between Will and his grandson. Robert was giving him a blow-by-blow description about how his best friend Danny knocked out Rocky Marciano in forty-two rounds and how

Billy could impersonate Marilyn Monroe better than Marilyn Monroe herself.

Flo was quietly chewing the inside of her lip, ignoring the food on her plate. Louise wondered why they never asked her about her job at the newspaper or her life in Vancouver. And she longed for her son to turn to her and tell her about Marilyn Monroe. She doubted her father even knew who Marilyn Monroe was — probably thought she was some new cashier down at the Five and Dime.

Louise tried to make amends with her mother and offered to make supper. Flo told her not to trouble herself because she had supper planned and anyway she was needing to get out of the house early so she could spend the evening at Mrs. Potts'. Louise wondered why her mother couldn't stay home just once considering she only saw her daughter for a few days in the summer. But what the hell, she thought, she left us kids at home with the old man every night of her life. Why stop now?

When she asked Robert if he wanted to go for another walk and then stop downtown for a milkshake, he said he had to go with Danny and Billy to the pool.

"Billy's mum won't let Billy be alone with Danny, cause she thinks Danny'll drown him. Danny's my best friend."

Louise realized if she didn't insist on having time alone with her son it would be like this until the last moment before they left.

"Why don't I come to the pool later and watch you for a while? Then we'll get in the car and go for a long drive. You haven't even asked me where the car came from. Do you know who it belongs to?"

"I don't know . . . Danny's dad?"

"It's ours. I bought it. It's second-hand but purrs like a baby and it's ours Robert. Why don't we drive up to Saskatoon — maybe visit some of your mum's friends. You can tell Mrs. Palmer we'll drive Billy home from the pool before we leave."

She turned to her father. Will Coutts hated cars. He'd never been in one and never would. "I don't want a word out of you Dad. Not a word. It's a perfectly safe car. We'll be home by ten. And you're spending the evening with Mrs. Potts, Mum — so you won't miss us."

Robert saw the car parked out front that morning but didn't think it was his mum's because she always came by train. Danny said it was a Chevy four-door with eight cylinders and a seventy-four horse power fuel pump in its engine and he could get her past ninety miles an hour with one hand tied behind his back easy as anything.

"That's our car? That's great! Can I start the engine? Can I? Can we take Danny? Danny'll go nuts. Can I take Danny?"

"No," Louise said firmly.

"How come? It's my car," Robert said firmly back.

"No. You go swimming with your friends. I'll pick you up with dry clothes. I want to talk to your grandfather."

Robert ran to get his swimming suit. Flo piled the dishes in the sink and said she was going to take a nap. "I'll do the washing up later and would very much appreciate it if no goddamn charity worker touches the goddamn dishes thank you very much ladies and gentlemen."

Will Coutts picked up an apple, a block of cheddar cheese and the salt shaker, as he always did after his midday meal. He sat at the kitchen table and began to roll the shape of his apple through the tingling senses of his fingertips. When he captured the exact roundness of its firm body, he placed it on the table and reached into his overalls for his jackknife.

He chose one of the many blades and paused to cut off a ragged fingernail.

How can he do that, Louise wondered? He gets blinder every year — it makes me nervous. And why do I feel him looking at me? I know he can barely see my shadow but I still feel his eyes — and his disapproval. He doesn't think I'm ungrateful like Flo, but he does think I've become ordinary. He used to think I was special.

Will Coutts cut into the flesh of the apple. Louise always marvelled at his confidence as his fingers danced over the skin and began to execute a series of expert slices that came to a halt just as the blade reached the core. One slice and pivot. Another and pivot. Tiny juice beads bubbling free onto his dirty fingers and the blade of his knife. All the way around. Then the finale.

He flared his hands apart and the sections of apple fell in defeat onto the table. Like a magician, thought Louise. Then he displayed the core triumphantly between his fingers.

Will Coutts always ate the apple core first. He said it was the best part because it contained a lot of protein.

Was she ordinary because her father was so extraordinary? Even before he was blind, she couldn't remember him doing things in a normal way. Her two older brothers still talked about how he made them spend an entire night raking the dirt outside their house. He made them rake the same stupid patch of dirt — over and over again. When the sun came up, he let the two little boys back in the house to meet a newborn baby. It was their sister, Louise.

Will Coutts took the salt shaker and sprinkled it across the table, knowing some would land on the apple wedges. Then he wiped the juice from his knife onto his overalls and cut the block of cheese into thin strips, the blade guided by the radar sensing at the tip of his left thumb. Finally, he folded the blade into the jackknife and put it in his pocket. He proceeded to eat.

I feel like a voyeur, thought Louise. Like I'm going to be caught and arrested for doing something unspeakable — for looking at my father — for daring to think that I might want to live with my son. He knows what I'm going to say. That's why he's ignoring me. He knows.

Louise watched her father take a piece of cheese into his mouth. He was careful not to chew. Then he added a wedge of apple. Just like an ancient lion, thought Louise, savouring the choice morsels of the kill, the young waiting at a distance to take their turn. He chewed. And chewed. And when he swallowed, his huge lump of an Adam's apple wobbled clumsily and betrayed the vulnerability of his age. A second piece of cheese and an apple wedge. A third. Then he spoke.

"You heard about the woman who was at that parade watching her son in the marching band? 'Look at that,' she said to the crowd around her. 'Every single person in that band is marching out of step except my son.'"

Louise knew what was coming next. Some lecture about the virtues of being different — how if people have long hair, don't be afraid to wear yours short.

She knew she had to find as much fault in her father as she could or she wouldn't be able to stand up to him. How about the one about the old fool who has the chance to get his eye fixed, she thought. All he has to do is go to the States for a simple operation? But he doesn't want to go because everyone's marching south of the border. Everyone wants their cataracts taken off so they can see the world around them. But not my father. No. He'd rather be blind and one of a kind.

Right Dad — get on with one of your parables about how important it is to be different. I'll take you on this time. I'm taking my son dammit.

Why do I feel paralysed in front of him? Why do I feel so dry in the throat? Why won't the words come out of my mouth?

"It's a funny story and we all laugh at that woman as if she's some kind of idiot. But you know, Honey, she might be right. Her son just might be marching to the right beat. Who are we to judge? And the only person who should be concerned is her son. He's the one who has to live with himself."

He hadn't called her Honey since she'd been a child. Damn him to hell, she thought. Damn him.

"And there's the other side of it too. You don't march different just for the sake of marching different, Honey."

"I have to talk to you about Robert, Dad."

"You march to the beat your conscience tells you to listen to. It just so happens that most of the time it's against the flow of the crowd."

"Listen to me Dad, please . . . "

"So you think about Robert. You look at that strong healthy boy and you know he's happy. But the marching crowd says to you, 'Hey Louise, you're going the wrong way.' You don't want us to think you're a bad mother do ya? And that's hard Honey. That's bloody hard. 'Cause I know you'd be happier marching with that crowd. Most people are. But what does your conscience say? It says one thing. It says: what's best for your son? It's not about your happiness. It's about his."

I'm choking, thought Louise. I'm choking. I want my son. I won't listen.

"And that damn car business. It's not the corruption of the profit-makers who'll do anything to make a fortune and don't give a damn about safety that worries me. It's not even them tin frames that'll snap out of shape as easy as a can of sardines when you fly into some telephone pole, or all that electronic hodgepodge that was wired in by some dumb union guy with an IQ of sixty-five and a hangover. Oh no, I'll tell you what worries me. It's those other damn idiots with IQ's of less than fifty who are out there driving over forty miles an hour not giving a goddamn about anyone else's safety. That's what worries me. You know we still got trains when it's too far to walk. But go ahead Louise. Take Robert. Just make sure he gets back in one piece."

Will Coutts got up and walked out front to pick up his wheelbarrow, leaving the remains of his apple and cheese on the table.

PART TWO

Robert sat on the window seat of the Saskatoon apartment and watched the two women and their Marilyn Monroe stockings clinging to their crossover legs — their red fingernails flicking at clouds of smoke and their closed teeth sucking at the air whenever they took a puff. All the while their high-heeled shoes were tap tap tapping to the rhythm of what Robert thought must be "Take Me Out to the Ball Game".

Robert's mother and her friend Valerie leaned into each other and talked. They talked and talked. On the drive up his mother told him Valerie was her best friend from university and that she had a Bachelor of Education Degree. Robert wished they'd just stop talking. He wanted to get back into their car and count the telephone poles between Biggar and Saskatoon. He thought he'd missed one near Perdue.

Take me out to the ball game — tap tap tap tap — take me out to the car — tap tap tap tap — buy me some peanuts and Cracker Jacks — I don't care if I ever come back — tap tap tap tap — talk talk talk talk. When are they going to stop talking about this Les guy, Robert wanted to know? So what if he's a bachelor on a boat? We could've driven to the Vancouver Ocean and back seventeen times for as long as it takes them to talk talk talk talk and tap tap tap.

Finally his mother got up and said she had to leave because she didn't want it to be too late when they got back. She said she'd keep Valerie posted about how it worked out with Les.

The Bachelor of Education woman held her chin up as if her head was above water and spun it towards Robert. She told him it was lovely to have such a nice chat with him and he was welcome back any time. Robert hoped she'd meet some good bachelor pretty soon who'd take her to work on a boat in Vancouver where she didn't have time for chatting. Then she said she had a special present for him.

She returned from the kitchen with a large tin. It had the picture of a spotted dog on the lid and was full to the brim with candies. After taking one, Robert replaced the lid and told her he'd try to make the candies last for many years. He felt sorry he hadn't liked her and hoped she didn't fall off the boat when she met her bachelor.

It was great to be back in the car, even if he did have to sit in the back seat. When his mum hit the accelerator full speed ahead it shook like a souped-up seventy-four power army tank. It was his — and it was a Chevy!

Louise figured it would take just over an hour and a half to get back. She was too nervous to have the conversation while she was driving, so pulled into a farmer's lane off the gravel highway. The sun was setting.

"We'll wait for the sun to go down so it's not shining in our eyes. Let's get out and see what's up the lane."

Oh no, not the meadowlarks again, thought Robert.

It's now or never, thought Louise.

"I want to talk to you Robert, and I want you to listen carefully." She took a deep breath. "I know you're only six, but even at six life can be complicated. Difficult even."

I know that, thought Robert. He already knew he was really bad at hockey and for sure that made things difficult. And he didn't even like hockey much.

"I'll tell you what's difficult for me, Robert — not living with you. That's very hard. So sometimes I bet you wonder why I don't live here. Or why you don't live with me . . . "

Robert started looking for the meadowlarks.

Get on with it, Louise told herself. Just get on with it.

"I know you've been happy with your grandparents, but sometimes things have to change. And just like it's been hard for me, now it might be hard for you for a while."

If only I had a sign, she thought. I have to know I'm doing the right thing. "Robert — I need to know what you're thinking . . . "

"Is that a meadowlark?" asked Robert.

"Yes by God. Yes. That is a meadowlark."

"It's beautiful, Mum. It's beautiful. Listen."

Louise and her son stood transfixed. Not a muscle moved. Not a breath. In a glorious instant Louise felt her son's heart beating with her own. She felt his wonder and his innocence.

They stood, tall on the prairie, and they listened to a meadowlark.

She looked over at her son who was still trailing the bird in the sky. She saw the perfection of his childhood. She remembered when she was walking through Stanley Park in Vancouver and discovered the most amazing baby bird perched on the lowest branch of a tree, barely above the ground. It was an owl, and almost like in a cartoon could swivel its head all around. It showed no fear. At a distance was a large cat, wanting with all its being to kill the bird, but for some strange reason not daring to move. She remembered the shock of power she felt suddenly from above. If she'd been religious, she would have described it as the power of God. High in the branches of a tall tree was the mother owl. The enormity of the mother's intention toward the baby was overwhelming. It could not be mistaken. She could see it — a straight thick line cutting through space to the baby bird. The mother could not retrieve her child. But she would kill with the fierceness of all mothers from the beginning of time if any harm should threaten its safety.

Louise looked away from her son. A meadowlark for Christ's sake. How wonderful — like a sign. Now I'll know what to do. And then I'll just do it.

Robert looked up at his mother. "Thank you for talking to me about hockey, Mum."

PART THREE

It was night. The Chevrolet roared as the road flung itself down like a magnet and sucked them through the flying gravel toward Biggar.

Louise was happy. She and her son were the only survivors in the warm blanket of the night — the headlights spreading a path to their future.

Robert knew his grandfather was waiting. His grandpa who told him that there was no end to the universe and there were things in the world you couldn't even imagine. His grandpa who said that eternity was forever and there was no such thing as the end of time.

Louise saw a loose pile of gravel coming toward her and swerved the car to the left. A hailstorm of rocks avalanched into the side of the tin frame. She swerved to the right. The tail end of the Chevrolet screeched forward and spun past them. She hung onto the steering wheel for dear life. Suddenly the road yanked itself from beneath the car and threw them high into the night. She called out her son's name.

Robert heard the long faint sound coming from a million miles away . . . rooooooooooooobert. And at that moment everything stopped. Time stopped. He felt his feet lift from under him and rise into the air as the Chevrolet twisted in slow motion. He saw the inside wall of the car pulling him gently toward it. He cushioned himself into the door.

Again he spun into the air, and as he began his slow flight to the other side of the car, he could see the tin of candies gliding toward him like a silent rocket. When it got close, the lid opened . . . and each candy . . . one by one . . . sailed out of the tin and into space . . . swirling around him like his grandmother's eggs.

The Chevy twisted and soared. Robert floated from one wall to the other. He knew there were things in this world you couldn't even imagine. His senses reached further and further   into   forever.   The   candies . . . the eggs . . . Robert . . . and a dog . . . floated over and over and over.

Flo was playing cards. Her grandson blasted through Mrs. Potts' front door and exploded the news all over her nice clean living room.

"It was great! The car went over nine times and landed on its roof in the ditch! It was great. Some guy from Rosetown drove us to the hospital and then he gave me a ride here. He's a baseball player for the Wildcats. He plays first base and said — "

"Robert," interrupted his grandmother. "Where's your mother?"

"She's at the hospital. She's okay. She's just got something with her ribs."

"What do you mean she's got something with her ribs?"

"I don't know. She's okay. Something with her ribs. It went over and over. It's a write-off. It's totalled. It's — "

"What about you? Are you all right?"

"Just some really neat bruises — look Mrs. Potts!"

Flo gathered herself together and ordered Gladys to take Robert home to his grandfather and stay there until she got back. She was going to the hospital.

Gladys put on some lipstick.

Flo Coutts pulled her great quivering flesh into a single muscle and started running the five blocks up the hill to the Biggar Hospital. Puffing and panting, she lumbered her way past Queen Elizabeth Park, the sign — QUIET YOU ARE NOW ENTERING THE HOSPITAL ZONE — coming at her in the distance. Even though she was sure the whale gasps from her throat and the drums in her chest were loud enough to wake every patient in the ward, she held her pace. At least if

I have a heart attack they won't have far to drag my body, she thought. I hope they got good beds.

"Where's my daughter?" she demanded, bracing herself up on the front desk.

Louise was sitting on a chair in the hallway waiting for her bed to be made up. Two high-school students were licking their wounds at the end of the hall having just beaten the shit out of each other. Louise whispered to her mother that she'd show her the bandages under her hospital gown when they got into the room, but assured her it was only a couple of cracked ribs and she was just in for observation. She related the details of the accident. The car was a probably a write-off, but hadn't turned over nine times. It spun out of control on some loose gravel and flipped them into a ditch.

After the nurse left them alone in the room, Louise started to bawl like a child. "How could I have been so careless? I am such a bad mother. How could I have let that happen? What is Dad going to say?" Flo waited until she calmed down and told her not to be so hard on herself. She'd take care of it.

"If the old man says just one thing I'll take his cod liver oil and lecithin tablets and shove them up his sorry ass."

PART FOUR

It was Sunday morning and Louise was up. She'd spent two days on her mother's lumpy bed — white bandages binding her chest like a wrapped-up mummy ready for burial. She'd been on the inside and she was ready to get out.

She pulled the iron out of her mother's hand and began to press Robert's clothes, careful not to rotate her chest or lean into the ironing board. Her ribs were still very sore. The only things that could move were her arms. It made her feel like some robot doll doing a Dutch dance in the back window of a moving car.

Flo sat down at the kitchen table and chewed her lip. It's her loss, she thought. Won't catch me doing anything for her again. Take the boy or not, it's her business. She wondered what kind of a butcher-job her husband was doing with his weekly shave in the bathroom. Maybe if she were lucky he'd slip with the razor and shave his bloody head off.

Will Coutts and his grandson walked through the kitchen and into the back bedroom. Robert had a sense of purpose written all over his face. He didn't even notice his mother was out of bed.

Louise kept on ironing. Finally her son came out of his grandfather's bedroom and said proudly that he'd pulled eleven pieces of toilet paper off his grandpa's face and not one spot started to dribble blood and that was a record.

Robert sat with his grandmother and watched his mother move her arms funny. Louise said she was getting all his clothes ready because she wanted everything to be fresh and clean when he started school in the morning. Robert had forgotten that tomorrow was his first day of school.

"I'm really happy I'm going to be here to take you to school tomorrow, Robert. It's important for a mother to take her son to his first day of school. I can meet your teacher and if I don't like her I can punch her in the nose."

Wrong choice of words, she thought. There will be no violence. If my son ends up like a little Biggar thug I'll knock his goddamn head off.

"Can I go call on Danny?"

"Go," said his mother. "It's your last day of freedom, kid."

The next morning Louise walked slowly and stiffly down Second Avenue, hand in hand with her son. They were ten minutes late for school. On the way back she bought her mother some new towels from Woolworths. When she arrived home, she picked up her suitcase and started to struggle down the street for the second time that morning, heading toward the train station.

She looked across the road. There behind his wheelbarrow was her father walking blind like he owned the universe. Louise bent her knees, careful not to twist her spine, and rested her suitcase in the loose gravel. She yelled across to her father.

"Hey you old bugger. Don't think for one minute I'm leaving my son with you and Mum because of some stupid story about a woman at a parade! I'm leaving him because it's better for now. And you damn well better take care of him. Because I'll be back, probably with a new car that'll knock your socks off if you had the eyesight to see it with. And I'll hold you accountable if anything goes wrong with him. So put that in your wheelbarrow and smoke it!"

And she marched her march to the locomotive heading west.

FLO'S PARTY

PART ONE

R obert sat in the kitchen under the sink. He was trying to remember something. His grandmother had told him to be home by eleven o'clock because it was Remembrance Day. She said she'd be mad if he forgot because at eleven o'clock everyone across the country was going to be quiet and spend a minute remembering.

HAP HAP HAPPY . . . IT'S THE HAPPY GANG. Flo's favourite morning program was on the radio.

Robert remembered. He remembered the time the plaster fell off the ceiling and landed on his head when he wasn't sitting under the sink, the time the black crow with a clipped tongue landed on the clothesline and said "Take a Powder . . . Take a Powder," and the time Mrs. Potts threw a teacup into the stove because his granny didn't see any tall dark strangers in her tea leaves.

BUM BUM BUMPA . . . IT'S THE HAPPY GANG. Usually Robert's grandmother sang along to all the songs and made lunch. Today she just sat at the kitchen table chewing her lip — her great granny body rocking back and forth as she looked far off into the cracked walls.

Robert tried hard to remember what his grandpa yelled when he tripped over a chair his granny left in the middle of the kitchen floor. He thought maybe it was "Goddamn you all to hell Flo," but then decided it might have been "Goddamn you to hell and back."

Flo turned to her grandson. "Today's the day we gotta remember all those poor soldiers who died in the war, Robert."

He'd hoped she was in a better mood and was going to sing "Today's the day they give babies away . . . with half a pound of tea." She always sang the pound of tea song when she was in a good mood.

"And your poor dad, bless his heart. Even though he didn't die right there on the battlefield, he still died because of the war. So ya gotta be very quiet — don't even breathe. Think of your dad and all those poor buggers who died just so you can play cops and robbers down at the fairgrounds."

The Happy Gang stopped their happiness and an announcer came on the air. WE INTERRUPT OUR REGULAR PROGRAMMING TO OBSERVE A MINUTE OF SILENCE IN MEMORY OF ALL THOSE WHO DIED IN THE WARS IN THE SERVICE OF QUEEN AND COUNTRY.

Robert took a huge suck of air. He could hold his breath for probably fifteen minutes at the swimming pool so this shouldn't be too hard, he thought. The only thing he knew about his dead father was that he was dead so there wasn't much to think about. So he listened to hear if anyone out in the town was cheating.

Flo couldn't think of dead soldiers. Instead, she thought of her dead brother who'd left her stranded with her sisters in a new country and gone off to New York City. He was the only reason she'd come to this godforsaken place in the first place. Sure as hell wasn't to be with my sisters, she thought. Happy as pigs in shit after they marry me off to some old man. Living the life of Riley with their young husbands. New houses. Red high-heeled shoes and hula-hula skirts. I hope Millie keels over and falls out of a goddamn airplane on her way to one of her precious little Hawaii vacations.

Robert's head grew very large as he thought about the big silence travelling across the country. He imagined himself dead with blood all over his T-shirt lying on the ground outside the bank and thought about his friends Billy and Danny being dead cops. He thought about the graveyard outside town. Once when he was walking the highway looking for pop bottles, he went in under the iron gates and walked all over the graves. He'd never thought about real dead people being under that ground.

He suddenly realized that people die. Someday, even his grandfather would die. He thought about all those people he'd walked on and felt sorry for their parents. He looked at his grandma. He wanted her to live — and he wanted to breathe so badly.

Here I am living in a dump at the end of the earth, a fat worn out old woman, moping over a dead brother I haven't seen for forty years, Flo thought. If my mother could see this she'd be ashamed. She used to say I'd be the lucky one. My granny saw it in the cards all the time. Millie or Anne weren't in those cards. It was me. She and my ma talked about how I'd be the one some young rich fellah would fancy — 'cause I had good luck. And a good heart, my mother said. That's what she said — "a good heart."

Robert worried that if this silent remembering went on much longer he'd probably go down with the rest of them.

Why'd she let my brother take us? I know she didn't want us to leave. Not me anyway — I was fourteen. It must'a broke her heart. It must'a just broke her heart. Flo started to cry for the loss of her mother.

Robert couldn't hold his breath any longer and started crying along with her. He cried for all the dead people in the graveyard, for the children who were gonna be born but didn't know they were going to the graveyard, and for his granny who must have known for a long time she was going to the graveyard.

When Flo saw her grandson crying under the sink, she broke into uncontrollable sobbing. She rocked back and forth to the rhythm of YOU ARE MY SUNSHINE MY ONLY SUNSHINE as the Happy Gang reminded all their listeners to tune in tomorrow when once again they'd be KNOCK KNOCK KNOCKING ON CANADA'S DOOR.

Will Coutts walked in his Canadian door and asked what all the bloody howling was about?

Flo turned on him, full guns blazing. "I'm cryin' for all the poor young lads who fought tooth and nail for our country and didn't live to see the light of day, ya son of a bitch. I'm crying because I'm rememberin'!"

"And I'm not crying . . . I'm not crying," cried Robert, not wanting his grandfather to hear the tears pouring down his cheeks.

Will Coutts had an envelope in one hand and a parcel under the other. "Angus from down at the post office says it's from your mother." He left the parcel for Robert on the table and went into the bathroom to wash his feet.

Flo realized there was no time to make a proper meal so she started on some grilled cheese sandwiches. Robert ripped open the parcel from the Hudson's Bay Company and pulled out the new skates his mother promised him when she was visiting during the summer. He looked at them in amazement. They were white. And they had sharp little ridges at the front. Robert tried to remember the conversation he'd had with his mother. He thought he'd told her exactly the kind of hockey skates he wanted. He was sure he said black. He put the skates back in the box and tried to remember. With all the practice I've had remembering this morning you'd think I'd remember black or white, he thought.

Flo, Will and Robert finished their grilled cheese sand-wiches. The envelope sat on the table between the pickles and the ketchup. "That's done with — now what's for lunch?" asked Flo's husband.

"That's it. I've been busy this morning. If ya want some-thing else make it yourself you old bugger."

"So what have you been doing all morning Flo? Polishin' the silver for when the Queen of England comes over for tea?"

"I told ya before — I've been cryin' for the dead boys. And I won't tell ya again."

"Well I'm sure as hell certain the boys appreciated it Flo. They probably all rose up from the dead, took one look at ya and decided it was better down under."

"Get out of my kitchen. Get out right now before I smash this goddamn pot right down on top 'a your brainless old skull you good-for-nothing bastard!"

"I wouldn't stay in your kitchen Flo, if it was the last place on earth. I'd rather be down under with the dead boys. I'm goin' — but before I do, I want you to read me this letter. Angus says it's from California."

"And I wouldn't read your goddamn letter if it was the last letter on earth."

"But he's blind Granny. He can't see with his eyes," piped up Robert.

"So let him read it with his goddamn stinkin' feet."

"Give me that letter Robert. I'll take it over to Lilly Cook's. She'll read it. She doesn't make goddamn grilled cheese sandwiches for lunch. I should 'a married her."

"Maybe it's not too late. Marry Angus and Mrs. Potts too for all I give a damn. Now get the hell out — both of you. Out of my kitchen. Go read your goddamn letter. I'm sick of you both."

Robert grabbed his skates and followed his grandfather. He wished he could read the letter. He'd just started grade one and was trying to learn as fast as he could. His grandpa said he had to learn how to read because he didn't want his granny or Mrs. Cook knowing his business any more. Robert could read some of the stuff from the stock market report in the newspaper but couldn't read writing yet. When he learned, he was supposed to read his grandpa's mail. And things like the funny papers and maybe the *Book of Revelations.*

Flo stood alone in her kitchen. She looked at the puke-green paint peeling off the walls — the paint her husband bought at half price because Harry Jessop down at the hardware couldn't give it away. She looked at the grease stains above the old coal stove, the linoleum turning up at the corners, and at the torn plastic curtains. And even though they'd only had indoor plumbing for a couple of years, the kitchen sink already looked like it was going to fall off the wall. She sometimes feared for Robert's head.

Flo walked into the crowded little living room. At least we got a piano, she thought. The Presbyterian Church was going to throw it out but gave it to her daughter Doreen because she sang so splendidly in the choir. Flo'd never been to the church, but used to love listening to her youngest daughter practise. It made her think of her home in Yorkshire. Her mother pounding away at the keyboards, her brother singing — always someone in the sitting room: neighbours, strangers, the lot. Not like this excuse for a house, thought Flo. The only reason people come here is to get their fortune told, 'cause they're too cheap to go to the goddamn gypsies. What am I talking about? There are no gypsies in this town. Just farmers and railroaders and layabouts. Could do with a few good gypsies!

My mum and dad didn't have two nickels to rub together, but they sure had fun. When was the last time we had a bunch of people in this house and just had fun? When was the last time we had a party?

Who am I kidding? I've never in forty years had a party. Not even my kids had a party — probably too ashamed.

Now my mother knew how to throw a party. The day after Christmas. Called it her Open House. Every year. All Dad's friends came from the quarry — and the neighbours; even that rich old bitch who lived in that big house across the village green turned up. "The dumb, the lame, and the blind," my granny used to call 'em. My mother started baking her Christmas cakes in September for that Open House. Now that was a party — my mother's Open House.

Will Coutts and his grandson stormed into the kitchen. "That busy-body sister of mine in Saskatoon has gone and written my brothers in California. Told them I won't go to Rochester to get my goddamn eye fixed — as if that's any of their goddamn business. The bloody fools say they're driving up 'round the middle of December. Drivin' up in the middle of winter for gawd's sake. They're bloody eccentrics — that's what they are. They're older than I am and they're driving in a car!"

"Figure skates!" Robert shouted as he threw the skates down on the couch. "Lilly Cook says they're goddamn figure skates!"

"There'll be no cursin' in this house," yelled Flo. "Any cursin' out of you and you'll go to your grandfather's room."

"I haven't seen the bastards since I was twelve and I sure as hell ain't seeing them now."

"Figure skates! My mother bought me figure skates!" continued Robert.

"They can snow plough their noisy contraption up and down Main Street till New Year's for all I care. 'Cause they sure as hell are not coming into this house. I'm not home to those eccentrics, Flo. I'm not home."

"My goddamn mother bought me figure skates!"

"Go to your grandfather's room this instant," ordered Flo.

"And now that snoopy Lilly Cook is gonna run around town telling everyone my business."

"She bought me figure —"

"Just shut up the noise about figure skates Robert," interrupted Will Coutts. "You're lucky you got anything. Who cares if they're red, white or blue? They're skates. You should be thankful they're a little different from everyone else — so stop your whining."

Robert ran into the bedroom.

"I'll tell you one thing Flo, if those —"

"And you just shut up the noise about those brothers of yours," demanded Flo. "I'm glad they're coming — whoever the hell they are. Maybe they'll make it in time for the party."

"The what?" asked her husband.

"The Open House. I'm having an open house on Boxing Day. You don't have to be here. You can spend the day with the bootlegger. That's if he doesn't come to the Open House."

"Well I'll open house for you right now Flo. Hand me the sledgehammer. I'll smash out the walls just in time for the deep freeze."

"I don't care what you say Will. I'm having a party. I don't want nothin' from ya. I'm just telling ya I'm having a party and if you don't like the idea ya can shove it where the sun don't shine."

Will stormed out. He picked up his wheelbarrow and headed down Second Avenue to the apartment blocks he owned on Main Street.

Will hadn't thought about anyone in his family for years. He hated his family when he lived with them and he hated them now. It was bad enough having a sister in Saskatoon.

When his father died twenty years ago, he started getting letters from his brothers, Matthew and Alex. They wanted him to forget the past and bury the hatchet. I know where I'd like to bury the hatchet, Will growled. Most self-respecting human beings would be dead by now — they must be almost eighty for Christ sake. Why don't they just sit on their expensive ocean-front property and make asses of themselves gawking at fancy hussies parading up and down in their fancy goddamn United States of America bathing suits? That's what most self-respecting eighty-year old geezers would do. Then kick the bucket with their peckers in the air and let the rest of us live in peace!

When Will got to Main Street he changed his mind about going to his apartment blocks and went over to the beer parlour instead.

He knew both Matthew and Alex had struck it rich. They went to California together, lived together and worked together. Neither got married but he heard tell they were terrible philanderers and left a trail of little bastards from the coast of Oregon down to the Mexican border. Along the way they gathered a fortune.

Will ran away from his family farm in Southern Quebec when he was twelve. The final straw was when his goddamn father took away his five dollars. He'd worked hard for that five dollars — walked three miles to school in the dark every morning for a whole year. Got there an hour early to gather wood and get a fire going in the stove. He hid the money behind a loose brick in a wall of their house.

One evening his father saw William sneaking a look behind the brick. He beat the boy black and blue with his belt and gave him some Christly speech about it being a sin to worship money. Then he snatched the five dollars from his hand — said he was going to give it to somebody who deserved it. That's when Will's brother Alex walked down the hall.

Will Coutts dreaded the arrival of his brothers. And he hated remembering.

PART TWO

The next morning Flo went visiting. She dropped in on all her neighbours up and down Second Avenue. Then she stopped by at the legion, the train station and the hardware, where she told Harry Jessop she might have to buy some stuff on credit and if he said one word to Will Coutts she'd drop over and have a nice chat with his wife, who might want to know about his acquaintance with a certain Erica Olsen over at the hotel.

On to the restaurant, the Five and Dime, the post office, the bakery, and the Co-op. Flo told everyone she met to pass along the invitation. Everyone's welcome. An Open House is an Open House.

She cut over and zigzagged up and down Fourth and Fifth. When old senile Mrs. Curry heard the news she thought for certain Will Coutts must have passed away during the night and gone to meet his maker.

After Flo slipped into the Presbyterian Church and tacked the news onto the notice board, she decided to double back to Third and have a cup of tea at Mrs. Potts'. It was the first time she'd been in the church and it made her feel a bit shaky.

On the way over, Flo planned her strategy.

If I start going to Wednesday night bingos I can add to the flour and sugar I win at Saturday night bingos. I got about eighteen dollars hidden in my underwear drawer so that'll cover the nuts and fruit I'll need for the Christmas cake. I'll make the biggest damn fruitcake this town ever saw. I'll do it just like my ma's. I should have enough left over to buy a couple bottles of cheap sherry I can toss in the punch — and if not I'll just cheat that old bugger at the end of each week when I read him the list of household accounts. By Jesus I'll need a lot of punch. And cake? Might need a couple'a cakes. Well I'll just have to do a lot of cheatin'. The old man can eat grilled cheese sandwiches for the rest of the month.

Flo told Gladys Potts she'd need to borrow her punch bowl and the biggest baking tins she could lay her hands on. She also listed doilies, napkins, eating utensils, cups and saucers, her record player — forget the records, they were all hymns, except for the Mario Lanza, she'd take the Mario Lanza — towels, her good tablecloth, a decent carpet, and a paint brush. Gladys liked the idea of a party but questioned Flo's wisdom of an Open House.

"What if somebody steals something?" Mrs. Potts asked.

"I ain't got nothin' worth to steal."

"What about my doilies, napkins, eating utensils, cups and saucers, towels, tablecloth, carpet, paint brush and Mario Lanza?"

"I'll keep an evil eye. I got the evil eye like a hawk."

"But what about all the riff-raff? Are they going to expect to come? The drunks and the prostitutes?"

"We only got one prostitute in this town far as I know. And she'll be busy as hell after all that holy family time."

Gladys heard from Lilly Cook that Flo's grandson had received figure skates from his mother. It so happened the church's figure skating club was planning a Christmas show down at the rink and there were no boys in the group. When Mrs. Potts told Reverend McDougall about Robert, he was thrilled with the idea of a boy joining up. The Reverend was still a bachelor and Gladys thought if she could do him this favour, he might come back to her house for dessert. She'd had him to supper a few years back but he was rushed to the hospital halfway through the main course because a chicken bone got caught in his throat. Gladys was a widow three times over and hoped the good Lord would be kind enough to deliver her a number four.

Mrs. Potts told Mrs. Coutts she'd be happy to oblige her request for certain items if Mrs. Coutts could get her grandson in the figure skating club.

"Done!" replied Flo.

Robert thought it was the dumbest idea he ever heard. He'd just got back from the rink where Danny's father had taken him and Danny skating. All the boys sat in front of the coal stove and laced up their black skates. Then they zoomed out, ripping over the ice, practising their fancy moves for hockey. Robert just stood there in his white skates with little ridges on the front holding the sideboards. Danny's dad said "skates are skates," but that's not what the boys said. "Skates are not skates. Those are figure skates." When he finally had the nerve to glide forward, the stupid sharp little ridges stuck into the ice and he fell flat on his stupid face.

Flo was surprised at her husband's response to the idea.

"Stop being afraid of being different, Robert," said Will Coutts. "Might be the only good idea that Potts woman ever had in her life. What else you gonna do with figure skates? Show those run-of-the-mill boys what you're made of — that's what you do. They're stuck on a team where everyone follows everyone else like sheep with sticks. You're marching to your own drumbeat — with no stick. They gotta follow the crowd — you don't follow no one. Show 'em what you're worth boy!"

Robert always found it hard not to follow his grandfather's advice. "All right," he said, "but I'm wearing a disguise."

He went into his grandfather's room and thought about how he could sneak down the street so none of the boys would see him with his skates. The only boy on the whole goddamn prairies who goes to figure skating, he moaned.

The next month was a busy one for Flo. She attacked the kitchen like Genghis Khan. No mercy, she decided. Chipped dishes, torn towels, stained tablecloths. Gone! Off to the unfortunate and needy! She packaged them up in cardboard boxes, but they only got as far as the veranda because she couldn't think of anyone more unfortunate and needy than herself.

She got Harry Jessop to such a peak of anxiety he did better than let her have paint on credit. He donated a can of orange and a can of yellow. Flo figured if she mixed them together she'd have enough and anything was bound to be better than the Puke Green.

She almost had a stroke one morning when she couldn't find Mrs. Potts' paint brush in the tub of turpentine. She thought for sure she must have put it by mistake in the tub of dried apricots, cherries, prunes, raisins, dates and figs she was soaking in rum for the Christmas cake. She was relieved to find it beside her favourite powder-puff on her dressing table.

Mrs. Curry sent the rum over with her nephew to help Flo recover from the death of her husband. She also wanted to know if there was a wake and was she invited. Flo sent Robert back with a message that the wake was at her house the day after Christmas.

Flo slip-slapped paint from one cracked cockeyed wall to the other, singing all the gypsy songs she could remember about broken hearts and fallen women. Although the results were a touch gaudy, they were at least cheerful. Flo dedicated the transformation to her fortune-telling granny.

The only time she took off was to go down to the legion to win extra flour and sugar at bingo. Her luck was so good she also came back with a box of Christmas chocolates. Eric Meisner, the bingo caller, commented on the attractive orange and yellow streaks in her hair and Lilly Cook said she was certain Flo had lost at least ten pounds as well as some of her marbles.

Flo taped together the rips in the plastic curtains, washed the kitchen window, glued down the loose linoleum and cleaned the sink, stove, and cupboards. Once the kitchen was ready, she picked up the baking tins from Mrs. Potts.

Will Coutts stayed clear — he had more important things to worry about than the shenanigans of his fool wife — and Robert spent the month trying to learn how to skate with one leg flung up behind him without falling flat on his stupid figure-skating face.

It was a week before Christmas. Flo'd lost another fifteen pounds and underneath her flabby arms was an unmistakable hint of pure muscle. She'd dragged all offensive articles from the living room and kitchen into the veranda. When that was jammed to the ceiling, she pushed her bed and dressing table against one wall of her small bedroom. Then she cleared the narrow storage room that ran from the kitchen to the back door. She lugged her children's trunks and boxes — full of the memories they were trying to forget — to the liberated space in her room. Just reward, she thought — once again back at the foot of your mother's bed!

Flo spent her nights in grunting dream-births, hauling and heaving the seven children out of her body into the series of squalid little bedrooms her husband had never failed to provide for her pleasure and comfort.

Waiting in anticipation in the coolness of Flo's temporary larder by the back door were three glorious fruitcakes, sweet replicas of her mother's Yorkshire hospitality, four dozen mince tarts, two rhubarb pies, six loaves of bread, three bingo bonus boxes of Christmas chocolates, and numerous tins of orange, pineapple and apple juice primed to mix company with the two bottles of sherry Flo managed to swindle out of Will Coutts' household accounts. Lording over all, from a shelf high above, was the pièce de résistance: the gleaming shimmer of Gladys Potts' punch bowl with twenty-four crystal glasses to match, the only souvenir from her first marriage to Frances Agnew, who got ploughed under by the train from Kindersley when he stopped his milk wagon on the railroad tracks to admire the slough.

Earlier in the week, Erica Olsen sent over a beautiful lithographed note stating "she was delighted to inform Mrs. Coutts she would be in attendance at the Open House." When Mrs. Potts found out the town prostitute was coming she asked for her stuff back, but Flo told her if she didn't leave well enough alone she'd tell her what she really saw in her tea leaves. She only hoped there wouldn't be an unpleasant backlash from some of the town's more horny holiday gentlemen.

The other bit of correspondence she got that week was a Christmas card with a picture of a near-naked hula-hula lady wearing a funeral wreath around her sorry neck. Goddamn sister of mine in her sordid little down under Hawaiian paradise, Flo thought. She had a good laugh when she noticed it was postmarked in Calgary.

Everyone was welcome at my mother's Open House, remembered Flo. The dumb, the lame and the blind. And this town is built on the dumb, the lame and the blind, so they're coming, town hussy or not. I'll even let in a naked hula-hula lady.

The living room was cramped but spotless. Flo's main concern was keeping it that way over Christmas. The piano had been polished every day for a month. She hoped it would make up for the fact it had never been tuned. She managed to squeeze a little Christmas tree in between the armchair and the coffee table. Mrs. Potts' carpet was in the corner ready to be rolled out on the day.

When Flo tested out the borrowed record player with the Mario Lanza, the old man yelled from his back bedroom to "Turn that bloody contraption off before I come in there and smash that screeching eunuch over his goddamn falsettic skull!" The thought of his brothers coming from California was making Will Coutts even more miserable than when the Dow Jones Average fell to a record low during the forties.

Robert's figure skating debut was in three days. He was about to make history as the only boy in Biggar to ever lift his leg more than a foot above the surface of the ice — in public — wearing white skates with ridges on the front and a Georgy Porgy Pudding and Pie hat. And to make matters worse, they'd made him the star.

He had to drag all the girls onto the ice behind him — by hand — and fling them all over the place until they got stuck into the shape of a horseshoe somewhere around the edges of the rink. Then he was supposed to zoom to the middle of the ice, everyone gawking at his boyness, and flash the girls with tricky figure skating stuff.

Arms wide — twirl in the middle — toe dance kick out — zoom zoom! Arms wide — fling in the middle — toe dance leg out — zoom zoom!

Then all the girls had to ooh and aah. But the worst part was next. 'Cause then he was meant to start showing off and skate backwards doing figure eights. And the little brats watching were supposed to get fed up with all his Georgy Porgy showin' off — Georgy Porgy for chrissake — and all their oohs and aahs got to change into booooos and arrrrghs as they chased him off the ice. Now was that a set-up or what?

Robert asked his grandfather if it would be okay if he chased them off instead. Sounded reasonable to him — so at least he had that to look forward to.

"But what if I fall? What if I skate out there, throw my back leg in the air and fall on my face?"

"Just pick yourself up," said Will Coutts. "And do it again."

"And what if I fall the second time? What will people think?"

"Who cares what people think — start over. I'm proud of ya Robert."

A day before the figure skating club's anticipated moment of triumph, all hell broke loose on the street outside Flo's house. A Royal Canadian Mounted Policeman was having an apoplectic fit in a beaver hat. He was screaming obscenities at two old heavily toqued farts sitting in a red Cadillac convertible with its top missing. Neighbours came from blocks around to watch the Mountie turn red in the face as he sputtered threats about "Saskatchewan fuckin' speed limits, fuckin' invalid driver's licenses, and respect for the fuckin' law!"

It had been the first high-speed chase of Constable Schumacher's career and his adrenalin was pumping. Sixty-five miles an hour all the way from Rosetown to Will Coutts' veranda! Schumacher was from Victoria and had been on the force for three months. He suspected he got Biggar as his first posting because he wrote poetry in his spare time. God he hated Saskatchewan.

When the sergeant from the Biggar police station arrived, the west coast constable poet was relieved of his obscenities and hauled away in another cruiser, re-confirming the onlookers' faith in the Saskatchewan justice system.

Flo made Matthew and Alex strip down to their long johns on the veranda before stepping into her clean house. Then they sat in the living room drinking some brandy Alex pulled out of his knapsack. She'd never met her husband's brothers before but they all got along like a house on fire. Flo couldn't believe they came from the same family as her old man.

Before starting to make grilled cheese sandwiches for supper, she made them swear they'd keep everything tidy for the party and not touch the food in the back hallway. Robert didn't know who those wild strangers were but sure liked the red convertible filling up with snow out front. Alex told him it used to have a roof thing but it got ripped off when they had to make a getaway under a garbage truck when they used to rob banks.

Robert tried to remember which brother was which. Alex was short and fat, and Matthew was tall and skinny. But other than that they looked exactly the same.

Will Coutts didn't come home for supper but Flo told his brothers not to worry because he wouldn't be able to stay away from his cod liver oil and yeast tablets for long.

Alex slept in with the Christmas cakes on an old mattress Flo borrowed from Mrs. Jenkins, and Matthew on a board he laid out on the middle of the living-room floor. He said it had to do with his back and something he was studying in a California cave.

Will Coutts tripped over his brother's body late that night and cursed a blue streak. He got out the next day, bright and early, and stayed away from the house all day.

Early in the evening, Flo, her nervous grandson, and her newly acquainted in-laws started the walk down Second Avenue towards the skating rink.

Robert was miserable. Where was his grandfather? Why wasn't he home all day? Why didn't he care?

When the four arrived at the rink, they saw Will Coutts standing directly in front of the entrance with his wheelbarrow, forcing the crowd to do figure eights around him to get through the main door. Flo told his brothers not to bother him with their concerns just now. Leave him alone with the boy, she insisted.

Will Coutts took his grandson by the hand and said, "You're head and shoulders above the crowd boy. You're marching to your own drumbeat and I'm proud of ya for that. I'll be right here waitin' for ya when you come out."

Alex and Matthew had the dignity to join the figure eights around the brother they hadn't seen for over sixty years. They passed by in a solemn dance and didn't say a word.

Robert zoomed onto the ice dragging his trail of lovely little six year olds and spun them into a horseshoe of pure beauty. He took a pause, inhaled the cold courage of the air, and skated fearlessly to the centre of the rink. Flinging his arms wide, he lifted his leg high above the slick surface so it was perfectly horizontal to the ice. Robert tasted the glory of success — and fell flat on his face.

He listened to the inner voice of his grandfather: "just pick yourself up and do it again." So he got up, skated to the corner, looked at the lovelies, zoomed back to the centre, drew his leg in the air and fell on his face. Again he listened to the voice: "just pick yourself up — who cares what people think."

Back to corner — quick flash — deep breath — lift — CRASH! Back to the corner — quick flash — deep breath — lift — CRASH!" Back to . . .

Then Robert heard the little lovelies laughing and the thunder of applause. And he listened to a new inner voice — "get off the ice so people can get home in time for Christmas you idiot."

Before hanging up his skates forever, Robert had one last go. He threw his Georgy Porgy hat into the stands, put on an ugly hockey face, and tried to bodycheck the little darlings into the boards, booooooing and arrrrrrghing all the way.

Reverend McDougall had to blow his whistle to put a stop to the chaos and Mrs. Potts swooned at the power of his tweet. The crowd went wild. They hadn't seen such a successful figure skating recital since Alma Perkins lost her sense of direction, skated full speed ahead into the boards, and landed on some Mennonite sitting in the fourth row.

"It was great Grandpa. It was great. I could have done it again and again and again."

Robert, Flo and the three brothers from Quebec went back to the house. Will Coutts told Alex and Matthew that they'd better keep their traps shut about anybody's goddamn eyesight or he'd get his grandson to bodycheck them all the way to the Montana border.

After half a dozen shots of brandy all round, the fighting was fast and furious. Alex and Matthew knew their brother had one chance to regain his eyesight and they hung on to their arguments like pit bulls. Nobody let up, through most of the night and all of the next day.

Finally Flo took charge. "It's Christmas Eve. I don't want one more friggin' word about eyes, ears, nose, or even kidneys out of any of ya. After Boxing Day you can rip each other's heads off for all I care. Tomorrow's Christmas. You can all chip in, give the boy a good time, and pretend you're

Christians or whatever the hell you're supposed to pretend.
Not a word!"

PART THREE

It was Boxing Day. After their grilled cheese and turkey sandwiches, Matthew and Alex told Flo they were taking her old
man down to the bootleggers for the afternoon. "Just to get
him from under foot for a while," they said.

"Don't bring the old bugger back on my account," replied
Flo. "In fact why don't ya just get him pissed, rope him to the
back of your convertible and drag him across the border."

Robert told his grandmother he was going across the street
to check out Danny's Christmas stash.

Flo was happy to have a clear run at the house. She told
Lilly Cook that her Open House would be open for company
anytime after three. She figured telling Lilly was the best way
to make sure everyone in town heard. That gives me a couple
of hours, she thought.

Flo took stock, said a silent Happy Christmas to her dead
ma, and flew through the house like a bat-outta-hell knowing
exactly what she was doing and in what order. She swept,
dusted, polished and scraped. Stacked, sorted, covered and
crammed. Opened, closed, flattened and fluffed. Then she hid
things.

She piled, tossed, soaked and strained. Lifted, stirred, loos-
ened and sliced. Unwrapped, unscrewed, mixed, poured,
tested, tasted, popped, doilied, and rolled out the carpet for
the gang — then she took a nip of sherry and toasted her
dead brother.

At about one-thirty, she piled on the powder and rouge,
wiggled into her smart lavender dress — the one she saved

for weddings and funerals — and looked at her image in the mirror. "Jesus Murphy, I look like I'm ready for a casket," she said in alarm. "Tight-lipped and all laid out for paradise. You're not going to church for godssake, Flo. You're havin' a party!"

She flung the dress over her children at the foot of the bed and pulled out her red blouse and the light blue skirt with the purple lilacs. Then she dug in Doreen's storage trunk and came out with her daughter's old makeup kit. She picked the deep-red lipstick and dabbed on a touch of eyeshadow. After choosing her largest string of pearls, a golden charm bracelet, and the full-moon silvery earrings that almost hung down to her neck, she looked in the mirror again. "Now you're ready for a party."

On her way to the kitchen to toast her gypsy grandmother before dumping the sherry in the punch bowl, she heard knocking. Who the hell's that, she thought. It's only a quarter past two.

In struggled Mrs. Cowley, the ninety-two-pound egg lady, carrying a carton of eggs. "Thought ya might need some eggs for your party," puffed the old dear.

Mrs. Cowley sat in the kitchen drinking tea. She panted away on her skin-and-bone's body telling Flo over and over again all the ways she was gonna be livin' the good life in exactly four months and twenty-two days. "I'll be sixty-five and livin' high off the hog — me and my old age pension," she wheezed.

Flo kept rearranging the mince tarts and sliced cake, wondering where the hell the people were. It was half-past three for heaven's sake. At this rate I'll be standin' here celebrating Mrs. Cowley's sixty-fifth. She'll be livin' high off the hog all right. Guzzling down my mince tarts and fruitcakes.

Flo heard a timid . . . tap tap tapping . . . at the front door.

Two elderly ladies she'd never seen before were grinning politely in the doorway. They were heavily rouged and powdered, and when they removed their wraps, Flo couldn't help notice their smart little lavender dresses. They introduced themselves as Mrs. Atkinson and Miss Flutey and said they were dropping by because they saw the invitation on the Presbyterian Church notice board. "It just seemed so Christian," they said. "And we're part of the Women's Christian Temperance Union."

Flo took their coats into the storage room, where she strung up the clothesline she'd hauled in from the backyard. The two ladies joined Mrs. Cowley for tea in the kitchen. Miss Flutey asked Mrs. Cowley if she accepted Christ as her personal saviour.

"I'm waiting for my pension before I can think about a personal anything," gasped Mrs Cowley. "Six months, Alleluia and Amen."

Flo was about ready to hit the punch bowl all on her lonesome when she heard loud banging in the veranda. She opened the front door to some tattooed thug towering above her in the doorframe.

"So I was down at the pool hall last Tuesday and Lou Leblanc was bein' hauled off to the slammer, poor bastard, and he yelled over his shoulder for me to come by here this afternoon and meet his girl Wendy. Said there'd be free booze and banana loaf. This town's dry as hell on Boxing Day and shit, who ever passes up banana loaf? Any of you's in there Wendy?" he hollered to the three teetotallers sitting in the kitchen.

When he reached in the air to scratch his armpit, Flo looked under the giant biceps to see Eric Meisner, Irene Henderson, John Hubbard and his wife Maureen, Lilly Cook, Harry Jessop, Clarence McIntyre with the walking stick he's needed ever since he tripped in the gopher hole, Sally Lafferty and her sister Shirley from Moose Jaw, Mr. and Mrs. Palmer, the Scott brothers, Mrs. Jenkins and her Pekinese, the Baily twins, Sarah MacIntosh, and the town whore Erica Olsen, all crowding into the veranda. Flo told the itchy pool hall hooligan to clear the deck and that Wendy was the one in the lavender dress.

"Well if it ain't the Happy Gang . . . SO COME ON IN!" she announced.

The Scott brothers got to the table before anyone and ate six mince tarts before taking their coats off. Harry Jessop slipped a bottle of rum into the punch bowl when Flo wasn't looking and Sally's sister Shirley told Flo her new paint job went lovely with her outfit. Lilly Cook said loud enough for all to hear that Flo's Christmas cake was the best she'd ever tasted, bar none.

Erica Olsen informed Miss Flutey that Christ was not her personal saviour, and the hoodlum from the pool hall asked Mrs. Atkinson from the Women's Temperance Union if she "put out."

Flo felt like a million bucks. Well mamma — we got a tattooed dimwit for the "dumb" — Clarence MacIntyre and his walkin' stick for the "lame" — all we need now is a "blind man." What am I saying, she panicked. Count your blessings woman — let's hope to God he's gravelin' south of Regina by now.

People kept arriving. Eric Meisner slipped a bottle of whiskey into the punch bowl when he was sure Flo was looking and winked his bingo-caller's wink.

Freda McConnell forced her darling little Marigold to sing "We Three Kings" twice. Flo put on the Mario Lanza before she sung it a third time. When Lilly Cook saw Sam Hodgenson trying to glimpse down Sally Lafferty's cleavage, he was so embarrassed he lost his sense of direction and sat on the Christmas tree.

Mrs. Jenkin's little Pekinese found his way into the back bedroom and peed on Will Coutts' wheat germ at about the same time as the Baily twins had to tackle the tattooed bruiser and pin him to the floor. He started raising a ruckus about someone promising him banana loaf and he sure as shit wasn't leavin' till he got banana loaf.

When Mr. Palmer spread the rumour that Flo's famous punch was going fast, Harry Jessop slipped in a second bottle of rum and Flo opened a couple more tins of juice.

At six-thirty Robert came home hoping his grandmother wouldn't mind he had supper at Danny's. He couldn't believe so many people could squash into such a small space. Rita from the Five and Dime tried to get him to dance so he hid out in the back hallway listening to Harry Jessop and Clarence McIntyre arguing something about Tommy Douglas the Commie Bastard and Dennis the Red Menace. Harry flung his arms around so much he got tangled up in the clothes-line.

People left and people kept arriving. The Happy Gang just got happier. Until about nine-thirty — when the party came to a dead halt.

Will Coutts lumbered through the door — pissed to the gills — his two bosom-buddy brothers holding him up by the arms. When they let him go, he staggered into the middle of the living room and teetered like an old fir tree ready to timber down at the first sign of wind. Everyone held their breath. Was Flo's Open House coming to a crashing finale?

Then he found his way to the piano bench and sat down. "Flo," he called out. "Come here my little darlin'."

Robert watched his grandmother chomp into the left side of her lip as she walked cautiously over to her old man. Then his grandfather did a very peculiar thing. He took Robert's granny and pulled her on his knee. The crowd almost passed out en masse.

"Do ya still love me Flo? Flo, do ya still love me?"

You could hear a pin drop. Flo turned beet red and looked up at her husband. "Well my ma promised me a blind man — so I guess you'll have to do."

Will Coutts started to bounce his big woman up and down on his knee and sing his one and only song:

"Daisy . . . Daisy . . . Give me your answer dooo
I'm half crazy . . . Oh for the love of youuu . . . "

The song was so out of key, everyone was relieved when old senile Mrs. Curry, all decked out in black, walked into the living room. She took one look at Will Coutts, screamed something about rising from the dead, and rushed back out.

"It won't be a stylish marriage
I can't afford a carriage
But you'll look sweet . . . Upon the seat
Of a bicycle built for twoooo . . . "

"EVERYONE . . . *Daisy . . . Daisy . . .* " And the whole gang started to sing out of key with him.

Finally the last houseguest strode through the front door. Flo was tickled pink to see her best friend Gladys Potts. After hiding the crystal glass Harry Jessop cracked when he was sneaking a third bottle of rum into the punch, Flo took Mrs. Potts into the kitchen to meet her husband's brothers. She was charmed and particularly impressed with Alex, who was engaged in conversation with the Women's Christian Temperance Union.

Flo's Open House whoopedy-dooed towards its conclusion. Miss Eleanor Pomeroy did a boogie-woogie on the piano while Sarah and Edward Moshinski, an old couple from south of Perdue, stick-walked over the carpet in an ancient pelican two-step. The tattooed thug from the pool hall finally ran into Lou Leblanc's girl Wendy, who'd passed out under the sink. He carried her out through the veranda and yelled over his shoulder they'd both be back in the morning for banana loaf.

No one knew where Will Coutts was. He'd disappeared about the same time as Erica Olsen.

When Flo took to the floor and wiggled her large behind in a sexy little gypsy dance with the Baily twins, people laughed and clapped. The bingo caller got so heated he hollered, "Take it off — take it off!" It reminded Robert of the black crow. "Take a powder — take a powder!"

Will Coutts' brother, Matthew, pretty well closed down the party when he stripped to his underwear and performed the yoga routine he was learning from some guy in a California cave. Alex, on the other hand, made Mrs. Potts' evening when underneath a swinging clothesline, in the light of a Biggar moon, he stole a little kiss.

Robert was proud as he watched all the partied-people pay homage to his great shaking granny before they filed through the front door.

"Same time next year folks. I think what we got here's a tradition."

Mrs. Cowley, the egg lady, was the last to leave. Flo thanked her for the eggs.

Robert lay alone in bed wondering where his grandpa was. Then he thought about the convertible and decided to be a race-car driver. Who needs hockey, he decided.

Flo sank into her lumpy old bed and listened to the deep-sea snoring of her brother-in-law in the living room. She felt the lush wet approval of her mother. She was happy.

The next morning Matthew and Alex stood on the street in their scarves and toques scooping snow out of their convertible, ready to rev their slip-sliding way through three-foot Saskatchewan snowbanks to the land of boardwalks and two-piece bathing suits.

"We didn't get too far with that eyesight business," Matthew hollered up at Flo, who was shivering on the veranda in her dressing gown. "So to hell with it we thought. He's old enough to make his own decisions."

"Anyway, I did what I came to do," yelled Alex.

"What's that?" asked Flo.

"I gave him something."

The two brothers opened the doors to the car and slipped inside.

"What?" asked Flo.

"Five bucks," yelled Alex. "I gave the bastard back his goddamn five bucks!"

THE NUDIE COLONY

"Did you see Lilly Cook's granddaughter?" asked Mrs. Perkins.

"Seen her in the Five and Dime for the first time since Halloween. Huge! Biggest toddler I ever saw and spoiled as anything . . . "

"I hear Mrs. Jenkins' old Pekinese made it through another winter. Must be twenty if it's a day," said Mrs. Baker.

"She was screaming blue murder," continued Mrs. Perkins. "Her grandma had to buy her a little doll so she'd shut up. Tiniest doll I ever saw!"

"If that dog ever passes on, the old lady will be soon to follow I tell ya. Last time I heard that little fellah bark was sometime in the forties."

"Can't wait 'till winter," sneered Mr. Switzer, the undertaker, when he saw Mrs. Jenkins and her ancient Pekinese alive in all their springtime arrogance as they walked past his front yard. "No peeing on my fence!" he snapped.

People all over town emerged from the long cold winter. It was spring.

Robert told his grandfather it wasn't fair to have to go to school in spring. Will Coutts agreed and told him to stop going until the fall. Whenever the grade one teacher from the Biggar Comprehensive School came to the front door to discuss this arrangement, the old man told her to piss off.

Robert spent the next two months following his blind grandfather and his wheelbarrow around town listening to stories about the four horsemen from the Book of Revelations, some great leader arising from the East, Armageddon, photosynthesis, and the teachings of a dead guy called Trotsky. He also struggled with the concepts of space, infinity, stocks, bonds, and why Mrs. Potts was a first-rate bitch.

When school was finally out, Robert was free to join his friends.

"Okay, I'm your best friend this summer right?"

"Nope. He's my best friend."

"Okay. He can be your best friend and you can be my best friend."

"Okay. But nobody's going to play with Paul, right?"

"Right. Paul's nobody's best friend."

"Okay Paul?"

"Okay."

"See ya Paul!"

The boys heard stories of tattooed gangs on motorcycles, riding into town in the middle of the night to beat up old-timers on the street. Robert and his friends decided they were the Daytime Gang, fighting to keep the town safe from the Germans, Commies, and the Voodoo Pygmy Queen.

"You're dead."

"Missed by a long shot."

"Got you in the eye — twice. Once with my machine gun and then with my machete. Right through your eye-hole."

"Did not!"

"Did so dirty German pig-snot."

"Did not!"

"Did!"

"I'm not playing."

"Wanna go swimming?"

"No. I'm not playing any more. I'm going home."

"Wanna dig a hole to China?"

"No. And I'm not your best friend."

"Wanna play war? You can be the German!"

"Okay."

"Bang you're dead! Right through the eye-hole, sucker!"

The summer was a scorcher and it wasn't long before the town began to wither in the heat. Lilly Cook's huge grand-daughter spent every waking hour splashing about in the wading pool Lilly ordered special from Mr. Jessop down at the hardware as neighbours confined their gossiping to the cool shade of other peoples' kitchens.

One particularly hot Saturday afternoon, Paul came racing down the street and right over to Billy Baker's woodpile where the gang was playing Pygmy Invasion From Outer Space. They were torturing Danny's little brother who always got to be the Voodoo Pygmy Queen.

"Hey Robert. Your grandpa's a nudie colony!"

"Get out of Billy's yard stupid gob face. This is private property."

"Robert's grandpa's a what?"

"A nudie! A nudie!"

"What's a nudie?" asked Danny's little brother, trying to pull the slivers out from under his fingernails.

"Naked. He's bare-assed naked!"

"Is not. My grandpa's downtown with his wheelbarrow making money."

"Nudie bum! Nudie bum!"

"Shut up! Shut up you commie dink!"

"Nudie bum. Nudie bum! Nudie Nudie — "

"Little commie dink-head! Little commie dink-head!"

"Mrs. Perkins called my mum and her and some of the neighbours got in Sam Hodgenson's new Chev to go look."

"Where? Where'd they go?" demanded Danny.

"The Finlayson farm."

Danny told them to shut up. He had to think for a second.

"Let's go," commanded Danny.

"It's over three miles."

"Go!"

Danny and his gang tore down the street out of town. "Robert's grandpa's ass is bare! Robert's grandpa's ass is bare!"

Robert went home and sat under the caragana bushes.

Bending and stretching his mammoth body in homage to the sun, the old man waved his tightly knotted six-foot frame across the horizon, silencing even the meadowlarks in its magnificence. The full length of the white beard growing from below his chin trailed behind the slow roundabout rhythm of his side-to-side swings. His huge arms and hands moved through the thick air as if conducting the music of the fields. When he ran on the spot, slapping his knees high up to the palms of his hands, jackrabbits sprayed a circular fountain of panic and ran for their lives.

Will Coutts took pride in doing whatever he could to maintain a healthy old age. He was blind — he didn't want any other inconveniences. At least three times every summer, once the prairie wheat had grown up to his chest, he'd find his way out to some farmer's field and take off all his clothes. He'd alternate between lying down and exercising in the sun, letting the hot rays fill him with the vitamin goodness his body needed to store for the long winter ahead. Unfortunately, this year Biggar hadn't seen any rain since well before the May twenty-fourth weekend, so instead of growing to his chest, the wheat stalks barely made it to his knees.

Edna Finlayson had just stepped off her back porch to dig up some beets when she saw the gruesome sight off in the left corner of her south quarter. At first she couldn't believe her eyes, but when the colossal figure turned around and the bobbly-bobblies below the giant's waist bobbled in her direction she almost passed out. Her husband wasn't home so she stumbled back into her kitchen and picked up the telephone. Sandra McIntosh, the Biggar operator, tried to calm her down and refused to hang up until the dear old farm woman poured herself a stiff shot of whisky. Sandra couldn't get through to the RCMP — the line was busy for almost an hour. In the meantime she notified most of her friends, just in case the Mounted Police were unavailable and she had to organize a posse.

Sally Lafferty stood between the dozen odd cars parked on the side of the road. "My Goodness, what's he going to do next?" she said to her sister Shirley from Moose Jaw. "It's almost indecent."

"I just hope he doesn't get a sunburn," replied Shirley.

"What's he up to? Martial Arts?" said the Baily twins at the same time. Sam and Orvil Baily always said everything at the same time.

His poor wife, thought Mrs. Baker. Poor dear suffering Flo.

Will Coutts stood upright, pulling his right foot to rest above his left knee. He held his arms out wide and was entirely motionless except for his head, which slowly rotated from the right to the left as he counted to one hundred. He had a particular fondness for this exercise. As well as being good for balance, it made him feel as if he was flying again like he did when he was a child.

"Who does he think he is, Jesus Christ on the cross?" asked Mrs. Perkins.

"No — it's more like a scarecrow. I think he thinks he's a scarecrow," said Mrs. Baker.

"Well either way — it's time for the old folk's home," responded Mrs. Perkins.

"I still think the poor old codger's going to get a terrible sunburn," worried Shirley.

"This is getting scary," decided the responsible Sam Hodgenson. "I'm going back to the car for my twenty-two."

Freda McConnell bent down to her sweet little daughter Marigold and told her to pull her skirt down from up over her eyes or they were going straight home this instant.

Just then a police cruiser screeched to the side of the road, spinning around two and a half times before landing in the ditch, its rear-view mirror knocking the twenty-two out of Sam Hodgenson's hand which shot a bullet into a cloud of dust.

Nobody could see who was shot until the dust settled at their feet and one unfortunate gopher was found lying by the side of the road with a bullet through its heart. Little Marigold screamed and pulled her skirt back up over her head. Constable Schumacher called for immediate calm and took charge.

Robert sat under the low prickly limbs of the caragana bush. Don't even have a real tree to sit under, he moaned. Nothing works. My father's dead, my mother lives on boats somewhere, my granny's a fat fortune teller, and now my grandpa's a nudie colony. Nothing works — even my turtle's dead as a doornail.

Two years earlier, Robert's grandmother bought him a little turtle from the Five and Dime. He called him Lucky. When he put the turtle on the kitchen floor, it would waddle across the linoleum and get lost under the fridge. Wherever he put it in the house, the turtle would find the kitchen and get lost again under the fridge. In November, Robert took the turtle outside to see if it could still find its way back to the fridge. Instead, Lucky the Turtle crawled under the nearest snowbank and froze to death.

Robert sat, squashed into the ground by the caragana, and cried for Lucky.

Constable Schumacher cautiously negotiated his way through the wheatfield trying not to alarm the blind old bugger, who was holding out his naked arms as if waiting for some extraterrestrial Martian to fly him off on a spaceship. Or the first prehistoric crane, thought Schumacher, waiting for the fish to put their new gill-lungs to the test and slide from the slimy marsh onto a wheatfield.

Alister Schumacher missed his home by the ocean. He'd never have joined up in the first place if he'd known he was going to get posted to the prairies. He hated the prairies. The Officer summoned his stability and stood a full ten feet away from Will Coutts, careful not to scare him. He'd hate to see the old bugger flailing blindly though the wheat stocks and end up scratched and starkers calling for mercy as he crawled through the spectators at the side of the road.

"Mr. Coutts. It's Constable Schumacher from the Royal Canadian Mounted Police."

Will was just finishing the last sequence of his balancing exercise, his left foot now above his right knee.

"Eighty-two . . . eighty-three . . . eighty-four . . . eighty-five . . . "

"We got something here to discuss, Mr. Coutts."

"Eighty-nine . . . ninety . . . ninety-one . . . ninety-two . . . "

"Am I coming in, Mr. Coutts?"

"Ninety-five . . . ninety-six . . . "

"Do you read me you stupid old fart!"

"One hundred and I'm reading ya fine Mr. Schumacher."

Will plunged his left foot firmly back onto familiar soil, and squared off his illegal nakedness directly towards the constable, as if in defiance of everything the law held sacred.

"Is there something I can to do assist ya, Mr. Schumacher? Are ya lost?"

The constable stared into the wheelbarrow that was resting at the midway point between himself and the offender. He was astonished at how neatly the old man folded his clothes, every article lying perfectly on top of another — the overalls on the bottom, followed by the shirt, undershirt, underwear, and crowned by the parallel curves of two uncreased socks, holding their place like boomerangs ready to be packed into a suitcase heading for Australia. The big boots stared at the constable in perfect alignment from the front of the barrow. Such care, thought the constable. Such symmetry.

"Are ya wantin' me to give you a lift back to town in my wheelbarrow, Sergeant?"

"I'm a constable Mr. Coutts, and it's rather the reverse. We've had a complaint. You see it's highly illegal to walk around naked exposing yourself to everyone in town."

"But I'm not in town. I'm mindin' my own business out here in God's pasture."

"I'm afraid its Mr. Finlayson's pasture, Will, and the town seems to have come to you. So the fact that you're engaging in the act of indecent exposure on private land, inciting an angry mob at the side of a major highway, gives me no choice but to have to place you under arrest."

"You Sergeant, are an idiot."

"I'm not an idiot you old felon, I'm a constable," replied Schumacher, taking two cautious baby steps forward.

"You stop right there, Mr. RCMP — or I'll ram my wheel-barrow right into your kneecaps."

"Do you need any reinforcements over there?" yelled the Baily twins.

"I'm adding that to the list of charges, Mr. Coutts — threatening an officer in the line of duty. You got no choice man. You put your clothes on this instant and march into that police cruiser. I'll guide you by the arm."

Will Coutts stood bolt upright. He'd never set foot in a new fandangled automobile in his life. He sure as hell wasn't going to step into one now!

"I'd hate to have to bring out the handcuffs," warned Schumacher, chancing another baby step towards the culprit.

Will took two giant steps towards the officer and grabbed the handles of the wheelbarrow, yanking them up to his waist. He clenched his teeth and leaned towards his adversary.

Schumacher thought he could hear a low growl coming from the old codger's throat and when the wheels of the barrow began to slowly rotate in his direction, he proclaimed his final warning much louder than he intended.

"YOU ARE UNDER ARREST YOU GODDAMN LOONY-BIN NAKED SASKATCHEWAN TRESPASSING SON OF A BITCH!"

"SHOOT THE BASTARD!" screamed the grade one teacher from the Biggar Comprehensive School.

The wheelbarrow began to gather speed.

Like a bullfighter knowing his time was up, Schumacher turned on the spot and started running to the highway. He could feel the horn of the beast ready to gore open the yellow streak running up and down his Saskatchewan-hating back.

"HOORAY!" cheered little Marigold, flapping her skirt up and down as she leaped by the side of the dead gopher.

Ripping through the small stalks of wheat, the wheelbarrow bumped its way into high gear, pulling the alarmed Mr. Coutts behind the enormous force of its intention, the equally alarmed constable yelling out for calm as the gawking mass lifted off the earth and began to glide like a vision toward him.

The crowd stood transfixed in unified awe, blood pumping wildly through their crazed and collective veins. Sun-scorched and splendid, they soared high above the prairie flatness of their everyday lives. The thrill of the chase. The promise of blood. Socks, underwear, overalls scattering haphazard in panoramic splendour. Aaah — summertime on the prairies.

Schumacher picked up the pace. The wheelbarrow picked up the pace. Closer and closer, the scalding breath of the bull seared hot on his chicken-heart trail.

Just then Paul, Billy, Danny and his little brother streaked up the ditch towards the excitement. "NUDIE BUM! NUDIE BUM! NUDIE NUDIE NUDIE BUM!"

To hell with this, decided the Baily twins, it's time for reinforcements. Orvil hurled his body toward the boys, who were about to crash into the oncoming wheelbarrow, and Sam dive-bombed the constable, who was about to meet his cruiser. The Baily twins always performed important functions at the same time, including eating, yawning, scratching and praying.

Paul landed on Billy who landed on Danny who landed on his little brother, Schumacher landed on the dead gopher, and the wheelbarrow slipped up the middle, smashing out the cruiser's left headlight.

Stunned silence overcame the appreciative audience. Eric Meisner, the bingo caller, had to stop himself from clapping and shouting for an encore.

The dust settled.

Alister Schumacher lay on his back in the gravel, arms outstretched, slowly rotating his head to check if his neck was broken. He counted to ten. The onlookers had the sensitivity to leave him alone — they could all laugh later at home.

The crowd acted responsibly, checking to see that nobody had any serious injury beyond sunstroke. Sally Lafferty's sister Shirley from Moose Jaw had been hit in the head by a flying boot but it just seemed to have made her a bit goofy.

Will Coutts stood unscathed and alone at the side of the road.

Finally, like a phoenix rising from the dust, Constable Schumacher found his last remaining thread of dignity and once again took full control of the situation.

"I want everyone out of here within two seconds flat or you'll all be arrested for interfering with the enforcement of justice at the scene of a crime. That means you too, Orvil and Sampson, once you get my car out of the ditch."

Alone on the highway, Will Coutts and his captor negotiated the fine details of how they were going to proceed into town. Will was adamant in his refusal to wear the Mountie's spare dress uniform and poor Mr. Schumacher once again had to enter the dreaded Finlayson south quarter to search behind every pathetic little shoot of wheat until he located the old bugger's entire wardrobe.

Siren shrieking in police escort splendour, the cruiser stormed a full two miles an hour through the loose gravel towards Biggar. Precisely twenty feet ahead, walking tall, was a fully-clad blind man, his large soft mass of shocking white hair glimmering proud in the late afternoon sun. And commanding the procession up front was the leader of the band, the wheelbarrow, plodding towards the certainty of justice.

Robert sat exposed under the stripped caragana bush.

He'd pulled off each of the long thin yellow pods and piled them in front of him. Then he carefully finger-nailed an incision down the inside belly of each pod, ramming the tiny seeds with his flesh thumb through the little yellow houses and out the other side. He didn't care that his hands were sore from the prickles when he yanked off the leaves. They weren't even real leaves anyway, he thought. They were tiny wannabe leaves. Robert had shoved his hands into the centre of the bush and whipped them back up the stems without letting go. Whenever he felt like it he broke a branch.

Robert heard the cars down at the end of Second Avenue coming back from the highway. He had just enough time to break a couple more branches before bolting through the front screen door and into his room at the back of the house.

He jumped onto the bed and looked out the window onto the junk pile in the backyard and thought about how the Daytime Gang was laughing at him and his grandfather — and how everyone in town had seen his grandpa's thing and that he'd have to stay in his room forever. And he couldn't even shut the door. It wasn't even his room. It was his grandpa's room — and his grandpa's bed — and he was looking at his grandpa's junk. And nothing was fair.

He hated the summertime. Maybe Armageddon will come tonight, he hoped. And the horses can trample Danny on the head. I hate Danny. He's a dink. I hate Paul too. I hope the fire burns their clothes off and they have to go to school forever — naked.

Nothing is fair.

Robert thought about his dead father. He hoped maybe his father wasn't really dead and when he saw the news on television about his grandpa being a naked nudist he'd decide to come home and rescue him. But then he worried that maybe he never really did have a father. And that maybe these people weren't really his family.

That would be a relief, he decided. Maybe I was just planted here by a spaceship to spy on them. My mother only comes to see me once a year. Most real mothers come more than once a year. And most real grandmothers don't tell the futures of people. Maybe none of them are real. Maybe they're Martians. Or maybe they're real and I'm a Martian. Or an alien. Maybe I'm an alien!

Robert's grandmother stood in the doorway.

"You're gonna have to sleep alone tonight Honey. Your grandpa's in jail. Supper's in about fifteen minutes. Then I'm going to bingo."

She looked weird, he thought.

Constable Schumacher told Will Coutts he'd be free to go as soon as the Justice of the Peace showed up from Rosetown. The Justice of the Peace from Biggar was bowling in Saskatoon. According to his lonely wife, Mr. Robertson was always "bowling in Saskatoon."

The police officer preferred staying with his prisoner to going home anyway. He dreaded meeting anyone on the street. And somehow he felt a strange kinship developing with the old guy — perhaps because they were both laughing stocks. It almost felt as if they were partners in the crime. Anyway, he sort of admired the old fella's confidence. Or stupidity. Whatever, he admired something.

"You're not a very good cop, ya know," said Will.

"I know," responded Schumacher.

"So why do something you're bad at?"

"Shut up you bastard or I'll call Rosetown and tell him not to come."

The constable sat down and began to enter the details of the arrest into a proper file. He was shaking. After snapping the lead on five pencils and cursing a blue streak, he got up.

Will Coutts asked the question again.

"Because I'm a goddamn chicken-livered coward," yelled Schumacher.

"Liver's good for you," replied Will.

"Because I'm scared I might be no good!"

"You're already no good."

"Because I want to be a poet."

"Ya mean you want to write poetry. Like Tennyson and Yeats and Garcia Lorca?"

"Yah. Yah. Like that. How'd you know about those fellas?"

"Just like anybody else would know about those fellas. Ya read 'em. I wasn't born blind."

"Well anyway — I want to be a poet. So why don't you have a good laugh. It's your turn."

"Who the hell cares who laughs, you ignorant young whippersnapper. Ya gonna spend the rest of your life afraid of being different?"

"I'm not listening."

"You ever hear about that mother who was at the parade watching her son in the marchin' band?"

"No. And I'm not listening."

"'Look at that,' she said proud as a peacock to the woman standing next to her. 'Every single boy in that band is marching out of step except my son.'"

"Piss off Coutts."

"Good for that boy I say, and good for the woman for supporting her son, although it's none of her business — none of anybody's goddamn business how ya march. As long as ya march to your own drumbeat."

"I said I wasn't listening. I'm going for coffee at the Chinese."

"Careful ya don't run into anyone sergeant. It's bingo night. Someone might start laughing."

"I'm going for coffee."

"Do not go gentle into that good night — "

"Shut your gob you old — "

"This is the way the world ends . . . this is the way the world ends . . . this is the way the world ends . . . not with a bang but a whimper."

"I'm leaving — "

"There was an old gal from Brazil . . . with a bosom as big as a hill . . . "

Constable Schumacher slammed the front door and entered the street, barely holding back his tears.

That night was the hottest of the summer. The town was restless.

Mr. Hodgenson dreamed of his new Chevrolet overheating and running berserk all through his house. It crashed into his wife's china collection and hissed steam into his bedroom. Mrs. Perkins gave birth to new kitchen appliances which immediately melted, the Baily twins — out for a walk in Mr. Finlayson's burning wheatfield — couldn't remember who was who and ran off in opposite directions, and poor Lilly Cook woke up to the pain of scalding tears, beside herself after watching her huge granddaughter shrink into a carton of Neapolitan Fudge.

Only Mr. Switzer, the undertaker, enjoyed the misty banks of slumber. He dreamt of two coffins resting on slabs of ice and heard a little doggy bark coming from the cold fog blanket of his pillow.

When the first ray of light hit the town, the creased and cranky opened their eyes, longing for the winter.

Robert slept just fine. He hadn't heard his grandfather come in during the middle of the night and woke up to the powerful legs scissoring away at the morning air above him. He looked over at the grimacing sunburnt face and reviewed his plan. His granny and grandpa were on the Inside World — and everything beyond the house was on the Outside. The front screen door was the space machine that zapped him apart and kabbammed him back together whenever he went from one to the other. The inside and outside were never to meet. Never!

Will Coutts swung his legs over onto the floor and went for the vitamins, minerals, molasses, cod-liver oil and brewer's yeast. I love my grandpa, thought Robert — but only on the inside of the screen.

When he finished his porridge, Robert ran over to Billy's woodpile where the gang were arguing about whether they were gonna play World War Three or Pygmy Queen Torture. Danny's little brother voted for World War Three.

"This is private property. You're not allowed," cried Paul.

"Yah — so take off or I'll call Constable Schumacher to put you in nudie jail!" hollered Danny.

"No," replied Robert.

"Yes," demanded Danny.

"And anyways — I'm Danny's best friend!" bragged Paul.

"Give him a bloody nose," ordered Danny.

"I'm gonna give you a bloody nose," threatened Paul.

"You're a dink," yelled Robert.

"You're a dink," yelled Paul.

"No I'm not!"

"Are so!"

"Anyways I got a secret," said Robert as he pushed Paul into the woodpile. "A big one!"

"What is it?" asked Paul.

"I'm not telling you stupid."

"Why not?"

"I'm only telling Billy and Danny."

Danny told them to shut up. He had to think for a second.

"Go home Paul," said Danny.

"Okay," said Paul.

"What's the secret?" asked Billy.

"You can't tell anyone 'cause I'm not supposed to tell."

"Who says?"

"The agent."

"What agent?"

"The secret agent."

"What's the secret?" repeated Billy.

"You can't even tell your mums okay?"

"Okay."

"My grandpa's not my real grandpa," whispered Robert.

"He is so!"

"No he's not. And my grandma's not my real grandma."

"Is so."

"My grandma's fat and my grandpa's tall. Do I look like them?"

"No."

"Who are they then?" asked Billy.

"They're grandparents."

"See!"

"But not mine."

"Who says?"

"The agent."

"What agent?"

"That woman from Vancouver."

"That's your mother."

"No she's not — she pretends to be my mother 'cause she's the agent."

"The agent of what?"

"The alien."

"Who's the alien?"

"I'm the alien."

"You're the what?" asked Danny's little brother.

"The alien. But most of the time I don't know I'm an alien because I'm a brainwashed alien. Just sometimes I know —

like now. If you ask me tomorrow I'll probably say I'm not. But it's true so don't believe me if I say I'm not — okay?"

"Okay," said Danny's little brother.

"When I go through my front door I get zapped up to space. Then I get electric shocks in my brain and they suck out everything they need to know about Earth. It hurts. And then I forget. And while they're fooling around with the wires on my head they put a body that looks like mine into the house. But that's not me. I don't live there. They're too weird."

"Okay. If you're an alien how come you play with us, huh?"

"Because I have to make everyone think I'm a boy. But I don't play with Paul okay?"

"Okay — if you're an alien then what's your alien name?"

"My what?"

"Your name. Prove to us that you're an alien by telling us your alien name."

"Okay."

"What is it?"

"My alien name?"

"Yah. What? What?"

"It's . . . it's . . . "

"WHAT?"

"It's Lucky!"

The Scarlet Bird

J ust my luck, thought Robert. First my grandfather gets found out naked in a wheatfield where everyone comes to see his thing and then I have to go to bed in the middle of the summer. Knocked sick in the head with the fever of a scarlet bird!

When he woke up in the dark room, his grandmother told him he'd fainted at Lilly Cook's and that he had a fever and was to stay in bed until he got better.

Will Coutts insisted his grandson recuperate in a pitch-black room because he didn't want to take any chances with Robert's eyesight. Flo explained to her husband that staying in the dark was for measles and you didn't go blind with scarlet fever, but Will told her that he was the goddamn expert in the going blind department and the boy was to stay in the dark. So Flo put a cot in the storage room at the back of the house. Then she hung blankets over the window and door opening to the yard.

The last thing Robert could remember was lying on his back. He was looking at a bright red bird on the ceiling high above him. When its wings stopped moving, the bird started to fall — slowly — like a spider on a thread. It landed on his stomach and fell asleep.

He'd been sitting next door in Lilly Cook's living room with his grandmother. He was feeling too sick to play with the gang but didn't want anyone to know, because it was summer and nobody should get sick in the summer. So he just sat and watched Lilly Cook bouncing her big granddaughter up and down on her knee. Boy was that a big baby. And the more that big baby bounced in its fluffy pink dress the bigger it seemed to get.

He remembered his head bobbing along to the rhythm of the bounce, and his eyelids getting heavier and heavier. After a while, everything got blurry. He couldn't see Lilly Cook anywhere, just this giant grinning baby, getting bigger and bigger — fluffy waves of pinkness galloping all over the room.

Then a large red bird flew through the open front door and into the living room. It started bashing into windows and walls trying to find its way out. When he stood up, he felt dizzy and wanted to puke. But he had to help the bird. He wanted to swoosh it out the door.

When the baby started squealing, the bird must have thought the pink waves were trying to pounce on it, because it got really scared. It got so scared it skyrocketed straight to the ceiling and smashed its head. Then it looped back up and smashed its head again.

That bird's crazy, thought Robert. It's gone crazy.

The bird slammed its head over and over — trying to bombard its way through the roof and escape from the flapping pinkness.

Robert didn't know what to do. He could hear the bird screaming and pounding its wings so fast it was even out-flapping the dress. The only thing he could think of was to reach his arms high in the air to let the bird know he was there.

When the bird saw him, it nose-dived almost to the floor. Then it shot right back up through the open space between his arms and flashed its wings across his eyes. He felt its red belly plop softly off his forehead. That made him really dizzy, like the inside of his body was sinking down the outside part of his body. But his hands kept reaching up towards the bird; he had to let the bird know he was still there.

Finally, his whole body melted into his feet. It was sort of fun falling to the ground so slowly. He remembered lying on the floor looking up. The bird was on the ceiling. When its wings stopped their fluttering, it began its long fall.

The scarlet bird slept on his stomach.

Robert lay in the darkness. He was sweating and every square inch of his body hurt. There was nothing to do but listen to his grandmother in the kitchen. She was telling Mrs. Jenkins about his aunt in Edmonton.

"Something's wrong — I know it. This morning when I finished my second cup of tea, I look in my tea leaves and what do you think I see? A knife. A goddamn knife, Mary. And those two kids livin' in that dump with that no-good hooligan. And Doreen runnin' around tryin' to make a life for the lot of them. Something's not right — I can feel it."

When Robert woke up later he was burning. And it was difficult to breath. He could see light sneaking around the edges of the blankets on the window so he knew summer was out there. And the backyard. He hoped his grandmother locked the door so nothing could creep in.

He hated the backyard.

Last summer when he was standing at the back door he saw a rat. It crept up from under some rhubarb that was growing between some sheets of twisted tin. Then it disappeared again. Robert heard it moving under the junk pile. It scurried everywhere. Then these two pink eyes popped out from inside a pipe. It had a slimy brown head with spiked teeth. The rat clawed its way over stuff and crawled towards him. He was too scared to run. So he just watched it come towards him. Over paint cans, broken chairs, tires, ripped plastic, and greasy old planks of wood. He wanted to call for his granny but she was gone. So he shut himself behind the screen door and closed his eyes. He pushed with all his might on the door until she came home. He hated rats.

The back of Robert's throat was dry. And the hot rash was scratching at his skin. He didn't want to close his eyes because he was scared of seeing a picture of the rat. He thought he could smell the rhubarb patch in the backyard.

Robert hated rhubarb pie.

Flo's voice came out of the darkness above his bed.

"I gotta catch the eight o'clock tonight Robert. I gotta see how Doreen and the kids are getting on in Edmonton. Your grandpa's gonna take care of you and I'll be back before you can say Jack Robinson."

Robert reminded his grandmother that he was sick with scarlet fever and it was pretty stupid to leave a sick boy alone with a fever in a dark room and a blind grandfather.

"I haven't got no choice Honey. Your grandpa will take care of ya fine — he's just through that wall. Besides, you got your guardian angel. Nothin' bad will happen to you."

"How do you know I got a guardian angel?"

"'Cause I got the gift — I know things."

"What do you mean you know things?"

"I got the gift."

"What do mean you got the gift?"

"I know things for gawd-sake! Like at cards. Or when I read tea leaves. Sometimes I dream stuff."

Robert told her he didn't believe she had a gift; she was just making up all that guardian angel stuff so she could leave. Then he coughed.

"You're gonna be fine. Remember what happened when you couldn't wake up? And poor Mr. Campbell got all crippled from the accident? Think about that. It's those two kids in Edmonton we gotta worry about. They're the ones who need the goddamn guardian angel."

Robert told her to tell his grandpa to keep the back door locked no matter what.

"I'll tell that bastard if he unlocks that door I'll burn his bloody wheelbarrow," she promised her grandson.

"I bet you'd stay with those two kids in Edmonton if they had the fever," he said. "You wouldn't leave them no matter what. And you probably won't even come back for my funeral if I die."

His grandmother's voice bent down further into the blackness. "You stop it. Those two kids don't got a guardian angel like you. Someone could hurt them. You're lucky."

He wondered how his granny knew that his alien name was Lucky.

"I don't give a goddamn if they got a guardian angel or not!" said Robert.

"Stop that ya hear me. I know you're sick — but I'm goin'. And I don't want to hear one more swear word come outta your goddamn mouth. Not one! And I'll know all the way from Edmonton if ya even think to curse. You wanna know how? 'Cause I got the gift — and besides, I know a little bird who whispers everything in my ear."

"Tell Grandpa not to open that door — and when you come back bring me a real gift — okay Grandma?"

His granny's voice flew out the door. "I'll be back Honey. Before you can say Jack Robinson."

Robert whispered into the pillow, "Shitty hell piss. Titty ass bum. Crumby goddamn Jack Robinson dink-head."

He held his breath and waited for her to come back and belt him.

"Ha!" he thought. "She ain't got the gift."

Robert couldn't sleep. He was too itchy. And he could hear the rat scratching on the door. I hope her goddamn train crashes, he thought.

His heart pounded out sweat all over the sheets and his rash started biting him.

"No I don't," he cried out. "I don't want her train to crash."

He could hear a train engine down at the roundhouse and thought about what happened when Danny's dad got smashed up in his train wreck. I was supposed to be on that train and could've been dead as a doornail, he thought. I could have got smashed up just like Mr. Campbell. Maybe one of those guardian angels was hanging around.

Robert could hear the scratching again and his feet got all tangled up with someone else's feet at the bottom of the bed. He stopped breathing and tried to make himself invisible so the rat would climb up the other legs instead of his.

He thought they were probably Mr. Campbell's feet. He sure hoped they weren't dead feet. He didn't want to feel dead feet.

When Robert closed his eyes, he saw the boat he was on before he woke up that awful morning. He wondered if maybe the driver of the boat was his guardian angel.

When Danny's dad had come to get him out of bed to go on the train, he couldn't wake up. Something was holding him under. That's what his granny said — "holding him under." He was dreaming about being on a big boat instead of in the engine where he really wanted to be. And he couldn't get out of the dream.

Grandpa shook me and everything, Granny said. Then when I woke up the train was wrecked and Mr. Campbell was all smashed. I bet even Danny cries now that his dad's all smashed.

Who drove the boat he wanted to know? Who drove the boat?

Robert felt hot and sticky. He kicked at the stupid sheets and tried to get those stupid other feet out of his bed. He hated dead feet. Then he thought about looking around the boat to see who he could find.

He would dream about the boat he decided. About the boat — the boat — the goddamn Jack Robinson boat.

Robert's grandfather was trying to feed him spoons-full of molasses and wheat germ in the dark. He didn't give him his medicine because Will Coutts didn't believe in medicine.

It was fun both being blind, thought Robert. He liked the feel of his grandpa's huge hand holding up the back of his neck as the spoon kept poking at his face trying to find his mouth.

"I gotta go down to the block this morning but I'll be back by noon. I'll make you some soup. Your granny talked to that fusspot Lilly Cook next door. I'll tell her to come over if you want."

"No."

His grandfather handed him a round metal thing that clanged heavily onto his chest.

"What's this?"

"It's a cowbell. I'll tell that busybody not to take one goddamn step into this house no matter what your granny said. Not one goddamn step unless she hears the clanging of the bell. So if ya need her after all, clang like hell."

"Is the back door locked?"

"Yes the door's locked. And your granny probably hired the RCMP to hide out in the backyard to make sure it stays locked!"

"I don't want to think about the bad things when you're gone. Tell me what to think about."

"No I will not. Nobody should ever tell anyone else what to think."

"But I don't want to think about the bad things."

"And if anyone listens they're a goddamn fool. People gotta think for themselves . . . "

"Okay then tell me about Armageddon."

" . . . problem is they don't know how. Can't think beyond their own two feet. They think the world stops on their own front doorstep . . . "

"Okay then tell me about photosynthesis or Trotsky or the world being round and how you can't fall off no matter what."

" . . . and the reason they can't think is because they don't have the imagination to know that things are different out there. There's a whole goddamn universe for Chrissake! There's no concrete block at the end of the universe Robert. Ya know what's there?"

"What?"

"I don't know, but it's not Saturday night bingo I can tell ya. There are things in this world you can't even imagine. But you gotta try Robert. And ya don't stand a chance unless you look beyond your own front steps. Think about that!"

"I'd rather think about Armageddon."

"I gotta go get the rent from that bugger Clarence McIntyre before the beer parlour opens."

"What if I get scared in the middle of the night?"

"It's still early in the morning for chrissake."

"But what if I get scared at night?"

"I'll be in the next room. Clang your bell."

"But what if you don't hear me?"

"Clang like hell."

A shaft of light shot into the room when his grandfather opened the kitchen door. Too bad he remembered to close it, Robert thought.

Robert didn't want to think about his own front steps, so he just kept still and felt the power of the smooth cold bell. Then he decided to put it down at the side of the bed in case he fell asleep and rolled over and made it ring. He lowered it to the floor, memorizing how far it was from the edge of the bed.

He thought about Danny's dad again. How he promised for months to take him up to ride with him in his engine. Just like he did that time with Danny. He was so excited the night before he tried not to sleep. He wanted to be wide awake when Mr. Campbell came to get him. It was gonna be great — much better than playing stupid baseball.

He remembered standing at home plate swinging at that stupid ball — and missing every time. "Just one more throw," Mr. Campbell yelled at the pitcher, and every time he'd miss.

He must have got to about strike one million. Finally Danny's dad told him to go to first base anyway. Probably felt sorry for me because I didn't have a dad of my own, thought Robert. Last time I'll ever play baseball.

Robert wondered what his friends were doing — if he had any friends left after being sick so long — and if they believed he was really an alien called Lucky. He wondered if maybe it was true. Maybe he was an alien — an alien with a guardian angel.

He remembered when he was sitting under Billy Palmer's woodpile and decided to go home. He didn't know why — he just wanted to go home. When he got up, this big hunk of wood came crashing down on Billy's head. And then there was the time when everyone at his school got lice. But not him. His granny looked in his hair and he didn't even have one. Not one. Must have been the guardian angel, he thought.

Then the stuff about the train. Yeah — he was an alien for sure. An alien with a guardian angel.

After they had their soup, his grandfather wheel-barrowed over to a café at the far end of town where they still sold coffee for ten cents. Robert fell asleep.

When he woke up his head was so heavy he couldn't lift it off the pillow. He had to force his eyeballs to slide down to the bottom of his eyelids so he could check on how his feet were doing.

At the end of his bed there was a man — a man in an army uniform. He was looking for something.

The soldier's elbow was leaning on an old fence that looked like it was burnt and ready to tumble over. But it didn't. His other elbow stuck in the air and his hand rested on his hip. He had really long fingers that drooped to the ground. They looked tired — like they couldn't even hold cigarettes anymore.

He had this weird hat that dripped over his ear towards the fence. And a shiny black belt hanging loose around the outside of his woolly uniform. A shirt collar was popping out at the top of his undone jacket like the wings of a bird.

There was a mustache under his nose and a smirk under the mustache. His head moved from side to side looking for something.

The ground behind him was burned.

Robert knew it was his dead father and that the man didn't know his son was there in the room with him. That's okay, thought Robert. Now I don't have to be afraid.

The soldier noticed a pile of boxes in the corner of the storage room. They were full of photographs and report cards and old Christmas stuff. He walked away from the fence and unpiled the boxes until he found an old tin trunk. He tried to open it but he didn't have the key. So he shrugged his shoulders, started to whistle, and bent down to tie up his shoelace instead. Then he walked to the back door to leave.

When he pulled up the blanket to get to the doorknob, light flashed through the cracks and glimmered on his shirt collar. He stared into the door for a long time, like he was trying to decide something. Finally he dropped the blanket and turned around, whistling his way past Robert's bed as he walked out through the kitchen. No light shone into the room.

He must have just walked through the door, thought Robert. Right through.

Then Robert heard scratching and reached for the bell.

He had no idea how many days he'd been lying there. The only time Robert was allowed out of bed was when his grandfather let him use the toilet. And when it wasn't nighttime he was forced to close his eyes and blind-walk his way through the kitchen and into the bathroom. Once, his fingers touched the hot stove and when he screamed blue murder his eyes banged opened and let in the light.

He sure hoped that hadn't ruined everything. This house can only take one blind man, he thought.

His grandfather fed him and put icy-cold lotion on his rash. It got all over his pyjamas and the sheets every time. Will Coutts kept telling his grandson he'd be right back as soon as he found that bastard Clarence McIntyre and got his rent.

Robert wanted his alien father to come back. He wanted to see if he had any medals or tattoos. He wasn't afraid of his father because he knew that he was good and dead. It was the alive things he was afraid of. He hadn't rung the bell yet, but there were a couple of really close calls.

Being an alien is weird, he thought. If I live forever and ever maybe I'll get to the end of the universe. Even though my grandpa says there is no end. Wouldn't it be funny if I got to the end of the universe and I found God was sitting there playing bingo?

Or maybe I'd jump off the end of the universe and land on my own front steps. That'd make my grandpa mad!

If I was an alien with a bulldozer, I'd bulldoze the backyard all the way to China. I hope those two cousins in Edmonton get scarlet fever.

Jack Robinson is a Bobinson . . . Jack Robinson is a Bobinson.

I'm bored.

I wonder if Mr. Campbell's feet ever get itchy? Maybe Danny's mum has to scratch them. I wouldn't scratch them. Maybe when Danny's mum gets really mad at him she just says no. I'd say no. That would really make him mad.

I hate dead feet.

It's so hot.

I wish I was on that boat. It's cold on a boat.

Who drives the boat I wonder? I bet it's my thingamajig. I know that dead soldier's not my thingamajig because he didn't look at me even once. He was probably looking for a new hat. I bet he wears tattoos.

I bet the captain of that boat's my guardian alien.

I'm so hot.

I want my granny to come back for the funeral.

Robert woke up. His feet were dead. He couldn't move his feet. He could hear dripping. Slime. Drooling out of the rat's mouth. The rat was chewing through the door.

He reached for the bell. It was gone. He tried to call for his grandpa but his chin couldn't pull his mouth apart. He tried to moan like a cow but the sheet wrapped itself around his throat like a snake.

The door started shaking.

The rat was hacking a hole through the door with its spiked fangs. Gashing its way through. Pounding its teeth into the wood.

Robert couldn't move his legs. He tried to yank open his mouth with his hands. He couldn't move his mouth.

Then he heard it. Cracking. The splintering wood. He froze.

A thin ray of light shone through the hole and fell onto his dead feet. It glowed purple like rhubarb.

Nothing moved. Then he heard someone whistling and for a moment he thought he was safe — until the door slowly began to swing open.

Robert could see the backyard. It was burning. Shadows of the fire swam across the bed and onto his eyes. He looked but he couldn't see the rat.

He waited. The fire burned and burned until all that was left was an old broken-down fence on a black field. He heard the whistling again. And again he thought he was safe.

Then a huge piercing scream came from the ceiling and the rat jumped onto his chest. He couldn't move his hands. The rat turned toward his feet and started to crawl slowly down his legs.

The dead alien soldier was leaning against the fence. He was grinning.

The rat's breath blew hot on his feet.

Robert heard the train engine whistling high in the air. Twisted steel hurled off the track and flew over the backyard towards the house. His grandfather's eyes stared straight at him though the walls but could see nothing. He heard Danny crying — Lilly Cook's granddaughter crying — and the two kids in Edmonton hollering as they hid under a table. Dishes were flying across their kitchen and turned into sharp pieces of bent metal that crushed Mr. Campbell over and over again until he was all smashed up.

Spiked teeth scraped over dead skin. Robert wanted to scream.

Suddenly his dead father stood away from the burnt fence and walked into the house. He began looking again. He went over to the piles of boxes and pulled out the trunk. He put his hand into his pocket and took out a key.

The key turned in the lock.

Biting. Biting. The rat started to bite.

Harder and harder.

The father jumped away from the trunk as the lid flung open — and from out of its mouth came the scarlet bird. It shot straight up to the ceiling just above the bed.

The bird flapped its wings so fast Robert thought the house was going to take off and head into the universe. It sounded like pounding rain. Then it nose-dived straight to the goddamn rat. It pierced its beak right into its eye. Blood smattering all over the walls. Then the other eye. The rat squealed and ran blind all over Robert's bed.

Robert jumped onto the floor and found his bell. But he didn't ring it. The rat was dead.

Robert felt better in the morning. He didn't need his grandfather to hold up the back of his head when he swallowed down his vitamins and molasses. He didn't feel like any old alien. He felt like a Super Alien. Like he could do anything. He had power. He had his guardian angel.

Robert remembered again when his grandmother called him Lucky. She knew his secret alien name all along, he thought. His granny knew everything.

Robert could hardly wait to get out of bed. He daydreamed about what he could do with the scarlet bird. He'd be invincible — nothing could hurt him. He had his guardian bird. They'd blast this town wide open.

They'd swoop down from the highest water towers on the prairies. First Batman and Robin. Now Lucky and Scarlet!

If there was gonna be an earthquake, they'd fly everyone to Saskatoon. Or an A-bomb? They'd blast it to the North Pole before you could say Jack Robinson. And then he'd get a medal.

Just me and my scarlet bird. And the Power!

He hoped it wouldn't be like Superman where you couldn't tell anyone who you really were. It would be awful to be like Superman, he thought. I'd want everyone to know. I'd want medals.

That night he dreamed of a flood. Water poured down the walls and started to fill up the house. He ran into his grandfather's room to wake him up. But he just kept on snoring. Something was holding him under.

Waterfalls cracked open the ceiling as he ran knee deep into his grandmother's room, long sprays of foam kicking high in the air. Her bed was starting to sink. "Wake up Granny," he hollered. But she wouldn't budge. "Wake up!"

Then Robert heard the flapping — and skimming along the surface of the waves was the scarlet bird. He grabbed onto his claws just in the nick of time and soared above the waves and into the pounding storm. Down below him he could see a boat.

His grandparents' beds sank into the deep water. "Go Scarlet. Go!" commanded Robert as he heaved himself up onto the birds back. With two swooping dives they drove down into the sea and yanked out the sleeping bodies, tossing them into the boat.

Robert looked through the storm to find the captain. Who's driving the boat, Robert wanted to know. Who? Who?

The boat sailed into the backyard.

Robert woke up to see his grandmother standing in a shaft of light coming from the open kitchen door.

"Granny — I think I got the gift. I had this dream. We saved you in my dream last night. Me and my guardian angel. We dreamt you were drowning and I saved you. Don't go near water — I know I got the gift."

"No Honey. You didn't dream about me. You dreamt about Mrs. Potts' niece Edna. Last night in their basement she tried to drown herself in Mrs. Pott's wringer washing machine."

"What for?"

"'Cause she was sad."

Robert thought for a moment about wringer washing machines and what Mrs. Pott's niece was doing in his dreams. Then he asked his grandmother what she brought him.

"I didn't bring you nothin'. You just told me you got the gift."

"Stop fooling. What'd you bring me?"

Flo reached into the paper bag she was holding and brought out a package of Crackerjacks.

"Is that it?"

"No."

"Well what?"

"It ain't from Edmonton Honey. It's from France."

"From what?"

"France. Your grandfather put cotton batten in your ears or what?"

"What is it?"

"I been looking for these for ever. And then I remembered. I was sittin' on the train and I remembered. They were with all that baby stuff your mother left in a trunk when she brought you here."

Robert unwrapped a silk scarf and found three little metal glasses.

"They're shot glasses. Your father had them when he was overseas in the war. Had 'em with him in the trenches. Used them to get good and pissed probably. Needed somethin' to keep away the cold and wet, standing knee deep in all that mud, things crawling all over his feet. Who can blame the poor bugger for havin' a nip now and then?"

"I don't know Granny. Who can blame the poor bugger?"

"So your mother wanted you to have 'em — to remember him by. But don't put nothin' in them stronger than orange crush you hear me? 'Cause I got my little bird, and it'll be watching ya like a hawk till you're twenty-one."

"I got a bird too Granny."

"Good for you."

"So what can I put in them when I'm twenty-one?"

"What?"

"The shot things."

"Coca Cola."

"Anything else?"

"What?"

"Did you bring me anything else?"

"Yeah — I brought you a good swift kick in the arse."

"What?"

"Get out of bed you lazy good for nothing. You're better."

"What?"

"Get out of this house. I gotta clean up that goddamn mess your grandfather left in the kitchen. I don't want you under-foot. I'll get you some clean clothes."

Robert jumped out of bed and stubbed his toe on the bell. He stripped off his sticky pyjamas, threw them in the air, and waited in the shadows for his grandmother. He could hardly wait to feel the sunlight. It felt like he'd been living in the dark all his life.

When his grandma got back, Robert pulled on his trousers and got tangled up in his T-shirt.

"Granny. I saw my guardian angel."

"Your what?"

"It's a bird. I got a bird like you."

"That's nice."

"And I still think I got the gift."

"Good for you."

"Can I go now Granny?"

"You didn't even ask about your cousins."

"How are they? Can I go?"

His granny sat on the bed and started to cry.

"What's the matter?" asked Robert

"I hate that goddamn son of a bitch. Next time I'm bringing them home. I'm bringing them home for sure."

"Okay Granny."

Robert got his T-shirt on straight and stubbed his toe on the cowbell again. So he picked up the damn thing. He ran through the kitchen, living room, veranda, and out the door into the fresh air.

The sunlight blasted into Robert's eyes. He stood motionless on the front steps, his eyeballs wanting to holler they hurt so much.

He squeezed onto the hard cold bell and clenched the muscles of his face, forcing his eyeballs into the back of his throat. He'd never felt such burning. He was on fire.

The universe was zapping him. He was caught in the power of the light. Trapped on his own front step.

Robert wanted his grandfather.

He lifted his arm and clanged the bell. He clanged the bell like hell.

DOREEN FOREVER

The phone rang. "You eat every scrap of that tapioca pudding or I'll come after ya with the wooden spoon," warned his grandmother.

What a joke, thought Robert, she couldn't even catch me with the wooden spoon when I was three. She's too plump.

He sat there and looked into his bowl at the bobbly bits of mushy little eyeballs creaming through baby sick throw-up stink. It was dead porridge gag-puke. It was disgusting. No — he wasn't going to eat this guck. Besides, it stuck in his teeth.

His grandmother hung up the phone. "Pack a bag. We're catching the two o'clock to Edmonton."

Robert sat on the train scraping ice off the inside of the window. He wanted to see what they were passing, but as soon as the window was clear it froze over again. So he decided to eat his crackerjacks instead. He couldn't believe his luck. He didn't have to go back to school that afternoon and he got to leave the tapioca on the kitchen table for his grandfather.

He couldn't remember his two cousins. A girl and a boy or something like that.

His Aunt Doreen came to Biggar to visit a couple years ago and she had these kids. And then this really great guy came a couple days later with tattoos. Really great tattoos. Snakes and knives and a devil and a couple of birds. They crawled all the way up his arms and down his back. His granny made him pull up his shirt one day so she could see what was on his front. In the middle of his chest was this tattooed heart with an arrow rammed through it. And words. Something like DOREEN FOREVER. Or maybe MAUREEN FOREVER. Whatever it was, his granny said she wasn't holding her breath. His grandpa said he probably had LEND ME A BUCK tattooed on his arse.

But these cousins of his? He couldn't remember them. Anyway, he thought, it'll be great to see if the tattoo guy's got some new stuff.

Flo chugged the train along like she was sitting on a big horse trying to get the thing to move faster. I hate the bastard, she thought. This is it. This time she's comin' home. We'll make a bedroom in the back hall for the kids. She can sleep in my room. I'll sleep in the veranda if I have to, but she's comin' home.

She told her daughter not to marry the no good layabout in the first place. Sittin' around in the pool hall all day. Talkin' outta the side of his mouth. But no — she knew better. Sixteen years old and she knew better. So we have another goddamn baby in the house, I told her. Who cares? I already had seven and Robert besides. But no — she had to go and marry the tattooed good-for-nothing.

The train pulled into the station. It was night. Doreen stood alone on the platform, her woollen scarf pulled up over her chin. Flo didn't have to guess what she was covering up.

"Where are the kids?"

"They're at home."

The two women shuffled. Flo knew what was coming next.

"Mum — "

"Don't say a word. We're getting those kids and this time you're coming home."

"Mum — "

"Not a word . . . "

"I shouldn't have called you."

"What?"

"Everything's okay now. I shouldn't have called you. I'm sorry."

"Is he back in that apartment?"

"Yes. And everyone's all right. Everything's okay."

Flo grabbed her daughter's scarf. "Show me your neck."

"Mum. Don't."

"Show me."

"Stop it! You're making a fool of yourself."

Flo stepped back.

Robert put on his gloves while his granny chewed the corner of her lip.

"Well we wouldn't want that would we, Dear?"

"Mum . . . "

"It's all right Doreen. I should a' known everything was okay by the way you were cryin' on the phone. What a fool I am. You probably just tripped over his goddamn fist when he was helpin' out with the dishes."

"That's enough."

"And those Edmonton walls, they bash right into ya when you least expect it. Robert say hello to your aunt."

"Hello."

"Mum, come home, you'll see everything is fine. We saved dinner. You can get the train back tomorrow."

"Oh no, I'd just make a fool of myself in front of your husband Dear. We can bundle up here on the platform. Besides, we already had a sandwich on the train and if it gets too cold we'll slip over and play some 'a that Edmonton bingo. What do you think Robert?"

"Bingo'd be okay."

"Mum, I don't blame you for acting like this — not one bit. I was upset when I phoned you. But I made a mistake — "

"Damn right you made a mistake. Five years ago when — "

"I know, don't rub it in. I'm an idiot . . . I'm not worth — "

"Don't."

Doreen took a second to gather her thoughts.

"Look — you were right to come. It's been awful lately, Mum. And I was upset. But I'm going to give it another chance. We talked today like we never talked before. Sometimes I forget it's hard for him too. It's like a sickness. He needs my help."

Flo rolled her eyes.

"Come and see for yourself. If you can't tell it's different this time — that he's really made a commitment — then we'll sit down and discuss how the children and I can come back to Biggar in a way that's best for everybody."

That's all Flo had to hear.

Flo had to catch her breath after the three-floor walk up. She was only thankful the apartment was close to the station.

Constance was playing bucking-bronco with her father and giggling uncontrollably as the pair of them rolled all over the floor. Daren was sitting on a cot by the window that looked over the busy street. He was reading a comic book and rubbing a lemon on his forehead. Flo could smell the meat loaf from the stove in the corner of the cramped room and heard loud music coming from next door.

Larry got up. He had a huge grin on his face as he stalked over to his mother-in-law. "So how ya doing Flo? Long time no see. Take a load off. I'll open a bottle of wine."

Robert was hoping she'd ask him to lift up his shirt again. He decided walking down the street it probably said MAUREEN FOREVER and that's why his granny made such a fuss.

Doreen took off her coat and went to check on the meat loaf. Flo deked by her son-in-law and swept her two-year-old granddaughter up onto the couch.

"So Robert my man, is Biggar still bigger?"

"What?" replied Robert.

"Bigger? Is it still bigger?"

"Biggar's Biggar."

"But is it bigger than you know . . . ?"

"I don't know."

"You do know."

"I'm bigger."

"I know you're bigger."

"Got any new tattoos?"

"Yah — I got a NEW YORK IS BIG BUT THIS IS BIGGAR tattooed on my wee-wee."

"Stop that language!" hollered Doreen, who was opening a can of peas.

Larry wrapped his muscular arm around the boy's head and twisted him to the floor. Robert threw a quick glimpse up the wrestler's T-shirt. He saw a flash of red and blue but couldn't make out the words. There was something new on his stomach though. It was an eye — a big eye — a red eye. This guy's so great, thought Robert.

"Your husband always make you cook with your scarf on?" asked Flo.

"Uncle — say uncle," squeezed the tattooed man.

"Uncle," groaned Robert.

"Now say Uncle Larry."

"Uncle Larry."

Robert lay in a heap on the linoleum.

Larry walked over to Constance on the couch and pulled up his shirt. He pushed out his stomach.

"I can see you Constance."

The little girl squealed in delight at the big red eye and leapt into her daddy's arms.

Daren kept reading his comic.

"Dinner's ready," announced Doreen. "Come get a plate. We'll have to eat on our laps."

"I wanna eat on Daddy's lap," insisted Constance.

Doreen asked Robert to take a plate of food over to his cousin. "I want him to stay over at the window," she told him. "He's infectious."

Robert carried the steaming brown gob of meat stuff over to the dim corner of the room. Daren was still rubbing a cut-up lemon on his forehead, his nose buried in the comic book, looking as if he was polishing his head for some secret mission.

When Daren lifted his face to take the meat loaf and peas, Robert almost dropped the plate. All around the sides of his mouth and chin were crusty little sore-bubbles — like glued-on baby puke — squeezing his puckered-up lips into a spit-gobber from outer space.

It's like he's got tapioca all over his face, thought Robert.

"Don't get too close," warned Doreen. "He's got impetigo."

When Robert looked at the pieces of his face that weren't covered in tapioca guck, he saw freckles — millions of freckles — and a tiny drop of lemon juice sliding down his nose.

"Put down that lemon, Daren," said his mother. "Your freckles will still be there in the morning. Say hello to your granny and stop being rude."

"Hello Granny."

"Hi-yah Honey. Don't worry so much about your freckles. Girls love 'em. Lemon juice just makes them sour."

"That's stupid," Daren said, saving the remains of his lemon on the window sill for later.

"You treat your grandmother with respect young man. Or it'll be more than freckles you'll be trying to squeeze off your face," threatened his father.

"It's okay Larry. He's just a boy," reassured Flo.

Larry bought a couple bottles of wine from the party next door and the family ate their dinner without incident. They decided to leave the cleaning up until the next day because it was already past midnight.

Flo lay on Daren's cot by the window and listened to the party. Constance slept on a pile of coats on the floor beside her.

Robert was crammed into the edge of the couch, pressing his feet against Daren's feet. His cousin was crammed in at the other end. Even though Daren promised to keep his face down in his corner, Robert was taking no chances. He was staying awake all night. And that was final.

Whenever his eyelids began to sink, he'd blast them wide open. But after about the hundredth blast, he lost the battle and fell into the dream he kept having about his dead father. There he was again. In his soldier uniform. Sitting on a black horse in the backyard, waving at him to come over. Robert tried to run into the backyard but couldn't move because his feet had caught on fire. Flames were shooting up his body.

When he woke up, it was still night and his legs hurt to beat the dickens. He could feel them straining with all their might, pushing at the feet below. Robert hoped like heck the impetigo hadn't spread down through his cousin's feet and up into his own legs.

Flo didn't sleep a wink. She just lay on the cot trying to figure out how to get her daughter and the kids out of there. She heard Larry get up and leave the apartment at about five.

When the street started coming to life below her, she decided to go into the kitchen and make coffee. Kitchen, she thought. That's a joke.

Later in the morning, Doreen came into the living room and saw the children still sleeping. Her mother was sitting in the corner by the stove with her hat on.

"Well dear?" Flo whispered, "Want to know what I see?"

"Mum, I just got up."

"You told me last night to come and see for myself. Well I did. And I saw."

"Ma, you saw a perfectly normal family. We had a good time last night."

"Normal Doreen? You think this is normal?"

"I think we're struggling. But at this stage in our marriage that's normal."

"There's nothin' normal here Doreen. You got a little girl who's hysterical she's so desperate to please her daddy, and a boy who's scared to come out of that goddamn comic book of his. And you better get that face seen to!"

"He's got medication."

"If ya think lettin' him squeeze lemon juice all over his face helps you'd better think again!"

"Someone told him it was the only way to get rid of his freckles."

"It's his father he ought'a be rid of."

"Mum, stop it. They'll hear."

"Where'd he go in the middle of the night by the way?"

"I don't know."

"You don't know?"

"No."

"Doreen, he's dangerous. Ya never know when he's going to turn on you again. And I swear it'll be the children next. Mark my words."

"He'd never touch the children. He loves them."

"Does he love you?"

"Yes Mum, he does. Hard as it might be to believe, I don't live in a loveless marriage like you."

"You keep a civil tongue in your head. At least I don't let myself get shit on like some people I know."

"Keep your voice down."

"No."

"Mum. I'm sorry. Really. But I've got to live my own life. I know everything you're saying comes from the goodness of your heart. But I'm just not ready to give up."

"It's 'cause I love ya Honey. It's 'cause I don't want to see you wreck your life."

"I know Mum."

Flo looked at the three children still asleep in the living room.

"Pull down the top of your dressing gown, Honey."

"I can't."

"Yes you can. Just pull it down gentle," coaxed Flo. "I know what's there."

Doreen lowered her eyes. Her mother began to unroll the high collar of her dressing gown.

"Daddy!" shouted Constance, jumping up and down on the cot when she saw her father open the front door.

Larry stood looking across the room at the bruises on his wife's neck.

"I'm sorry Doreen. I really am. It'll never happen again," he promised.

"You don't get marks like this on your neck from runnin' into walls ya bastard," flared Flo.

"I'm sorry Flo. I don't blame you for what you're thinking."

"Mum — I told you to stay out of it," warned Doreen.

"Daddy. Daddy. Look at me!" continued Constance.

"Flo. I promise I won't do anything to hurt your daughter again."

"Bullshit."

"Mum . . . please . . . "

"Tummy eye, Daddy! Show me your tummy. Show me the eye!"

"Shut up!" Doreen screamed at her daughter. "Just shut up!"

Robert tried to disappear into the couch. Constance started to cry.

"Now look what you did," Larry said to his wife.

Constance cried even louder. Then Daren got into the act.

"Just fucking shut up!" he hollered at his sister.

"Watch your mouth boy," said Larry.

Constance grabbed the lemon from the window sill and threw it across the room.

"I hate you Constance!" yelled Daren.

Flo reached to pick the lemon off the floor, but Daren ran over and snatched it from her hand.

"Give me that goddamn lemon you little troublemaker," said his father.

"No."

"Give it here!"

"No."

Larry grabbed his son's arm and tried to yank it from his tight grip. Daren refused to let go. They struggled, Larry trying as hard as he could to pry open the white-knuckled fingers. Finally he wrenched it from the hand and hurled his son across the room.

Doreen screamed. Daren slammed against the wall. Larry stopped.

"I hate this goddamn fucking shit," Larry said under his breath.

It was quiet.

Flo watched her grandson crawl to behind the couch with Robert. Then she looked at her daughter, who was hardly breathing she was so still. Flo knew it could only get worse. She walked over to her little granddaughter and picked her up. Then she put her hand over the child's eyes and hummed into her ear so she couldn't hear what was coming next.

"I hate this goddamn fucking shit!" exploded Larry.

Doreen started throwing things. Anything she could find — an ashtray — a cup — the pile of dirty dishes from the night before. When Constance started bawling again, Daren joined in with her.

"Fucking shit. This is fucking shit," repeated Larry.

Robert didn't know what was worse. The dishes flying over his head, his cousins howling like maniacs, or the blood streaming down the impetigo on the freckled face beside him.

Flo hummed louder.

Doreen knocked down the toaster — the coffee pot. She overturned the table.

Blood's the worst, decided Robert, and he held his outer-space cousin by the hand.

When Doreen finished, she sat on the floor. She didn't look at anybody. She just sat on the floor.

"This is your fault you interfering bitch," Larry said to Flo. He turned and walked toward the door. "When I come back I want your fat ass out of here."

Flo held onto her granddaughter and ran over to the boys. "I think it's just a bloody nose," Robert told her.

"Lie on that couch and keep your nose in the air," she commanded, handing Daren some toilet paper from her pocket.

"Robert, hold the baby."

This kid's too big to be a baby, he thought. I wanna take care of Daren.

Flo walked to the centre of the room and rooted herself into the linoleum, surveying the damage. She looked back at the children.

"Don't move and no cryin'," she said with great authority.

She picked Doreen up by the arm and ordered her into the bathroom to wash her face. Then she pulled two cases out of the bedroom closet and filled them with Doreen's clothes. When Daren yelled out that he had to take a pee, she told him to "hold it." She walked into the living room with another suitcase and threw in whatever she could see that belonged to the children. Then she went for the toothbrushes. When the bags were lined up at the front door, she made Doreen stick out her arms so she could put her coat on for her.

"Stand up," Flo said to her grandchildren.

"Gotta pee," whined Daren.

"No time," responded his granny.

She put coats on the kids, handed Robert one of the suitcases, placed Constance in her mother's arms, picked up the two remaining suitcases, and all five of them walked out of that cramped and squalid apartment, down the street, directly to the train station. Robert was glad to get out of there. He was just sorry he hadn't seen what the words were scribbled over his uncle's heart.

Flo stomped over to the man behind the ticket counter and said she had a pass. The man said the pass wouldn't do for everybody. Her great quivering flesh seemed to come together into a single muscle as she looked the CNR man straight in the eyes.

"It bloody well better do! My husband lost his arm working for your goddamn choo-choo company!"

The man said okay and gave her five tickets; the train for Biggar was leaving later that afternoon at five-thirty. Flo was glad it left at five-thirty. It was the middle of winter so it would already be dark.

She turned on her heel and marched across the street to the hotel. She couldn't believe she'd called the Canadian National Railway a choo-choo company. She figured she must be capable of anything. Nothing would stop her this time.

They walked into the lobby and Flo informed the manager she didn't want a room; she just wanted to stand in the hall on the second floor for a couple hours.

And that's what they did. Nobody took their coats off. They just stood in a very dim hallway — with their coats on — and waited.

Whenever Daren started to whimper, Flo would shush him with a fierce little doggy bark. Doreen sighed. Constance slept. And Robert wondered if impetigo grew in the dark.

Their bodies stiffened with a silence that grew louder as the time passed. The air reeked of old sweat and cigarette smoke, its mustiness catching in their throats. But no one dared cough. They waited.

Flo didn't mind standing in the hallway. After that party next door and all the ruckus in the morning, she needed the quiet. And time would pass. It always did.

Robert tried not to feel scared. But he listened for any suspicious sounds. Just in case.

Every once in a while a creak in the wooden floorboards crept up Doreen's legs and sent shudders through her spine. She remembered how afraid she used to be of the boogyman when she was a little girl.

Only once did Daren say he had to pee. And only once did his grandmother have to tell him there are times when you simply have to hang on.

They stood in the dark, waiting for the night.

Flo felt strangely powerful. Her breathing reached way down past her rib cage. She could feel the muscles in her tummy. Her heartbeat slowed. She felt light. Awake.

Doreen tightened her resolve by drawing horrible images in her mind of what her husband did in the middle of the nights when he left her. She didn't want to feel sorry for him when he discovered her betrayal.

Daren thought about lemons and tried to plan the perfect crime. "First I'll tell the grocery guy I'm shopping for my mum. Then I'll look at the bananas," he began.

Constance dreamed of her daddy swinging her high above his head.

Robert thought he could hear a black horse at the end of the hall.

The sounds of the steam engines grew further and further away.

They waited.

Flo loved the stillness. The quiet. The uncertainty that her life existed outside the hallway. She breathed through her swollen ankles and into the floorboards. Her body began to fall away. She gave into the sensation of rising . . . of being lifted above her unhappiness . . . of entering a welcoming lightness.

She rose to the ceiling. And above. She was free. Weightless. Young. Far in the distance she saw green grass. She flew over the heads of her two aging sisters and their comfortable little homes. Past her ancient husband, the old man her sisters had made her marry in the first place. Past Biggar and the foreign prairie land she'd spent forty years of her life trying to like. Past a loveless marriage. Poverty and boredom. Past effort.

She flew to her dead brother in New York and rested him on her slim tight stomach. She stretched her arms to the sky and sailed on her back across the ocean. Home. With the darling boy. The one she loved. Home to Yorkshire and her mother and father. To her gypsy granny and the fourteen-year-old girl who was really her.

Doreen began to think about the red eye. She looked into the darkness above her. She could feel it everywhere.

Robert suddenly thought he could hear the shuffling of hooves. He turned and looked into the deep shadows.

Daren carried on with the details of his crime. "First I'll knock over a pile of pork an' beans," he decided. "Then I'll tell the guy some ol' lady knocked over a bunch of cans — he'll go over to pick them up — and that's when I'll head over towards the lemons."

Robert started to panic — "It's kicking up the floorboards."

Daren kept on plotting — "I'll go running down the aisles."

"It's galloping towards me."

"Past the cereals."

"It's getting closer!"

"Past the cinnamon buns."

"Closer!"

"The crackers . . . the vegetables."

"I see you . . . I can see you."

"It's gonna trample . . . gonna trample . . . "

"And there they are . . . "

"So I throw myself on the horse's back."

"I shove in my hands."

"We gallop down the hallway." "I fill my pockets full." "The black horse leaps through the flames of a burning door." "I take off into the street." "And there he is . . . "

"I can see you Doreen."

"My dead father!"

A bolt of light shot down the hallway onto their faces.

A nervous young couple stood in the half-shadow. They didn't know whether to go into the crowded hallway or shut the door and go back to their room.

"My mum'll kill me if I don't get home for dinner," the young woman whispered to her boyfriend.

Can't be more that sixteen, thought Flo, as she asked them the time.

"About five," muttered the boy, shutting the door in embarrassment.

"We're goin'," Flo informed the shadows next to her. "Follow me, and I don't want no slowpokes."

They walked down the stairs, thanked the hotel manager, and went across to the train station. It was dark. The train had just come in.

Larry stood on the platform. Tears were filling his eyes. He went over to Doreen and tried to kiss her. Doreen ducked under his arms and handed Constance to the conductor who was standing on the boarding box. Then she pulled the two boys up the steps and disappeared into the passenger car. Flo was left with the three suitcases, standing between Larry and the train.

He started to walk towards her. Flo lifted her wobbling index finger and met him halfway. She could hear Constance crying somewhere behind her.

"You big fat interfering bitch," he said.

"I'll slap your face if you take one more step towards that train," she warned. "I'll slap you silly."

"Why don't you mind you own business for once in your life?"

"Hitting my daughter is my business," she fumed, her finger shaking up and down like a weapon ready to go off.

He stopped. Flo looked behind her. Doreen had come off the train with her children.

A long piercing whistle steamed out of the engine. The conductor told Flo she had to hurry.

Flo looked towards her daughter, but Doreen buried her face into her coat and pulled the kids towards her husband. Constance jumped into her daddy's arms. Daren ran into the station to pee.

"This train's pulling out Ma'am," stressed the conductor, who was standing beside Robert above the boarding box between the cars. "Get those suitcases aboard or get them out of here. They're too close to the track."

Flo thought for a moment. Then she walked around the suitcases and stepped onto the locomotive. The conductor pulled up the boarding box.

Larry handed Constance to his wife, walked towards the train, and bent down to pick up the cases. He heard Robert mumbling something at him from above.

Doreen lifted her face to her mother and Flo looked into her daughter's eyes. She drew them to her with all of her strength. With the power of lightness.

Robert mumbled again.

"What did you say Robert, my man?" asked Larry.

The train jerked forward, preparing to move.

"What you say?" Larry asked again.

"I said what's in your heart?"

"What?"

"He ain't got no heart," Flo told her grandson.

"Yes I do," Larry responded.

"No you don't ya heartless son-of-a-bitch. You're scum of the earth!" hollered Flo, as the train started to chug slowly down the platform.

Robert was determined to get an answer to his question.
"Have you got a heart or not?" he called out one last time.

"Oh. My heart!" Larry yelled back at the boy.

"Yah!"

The train was picking up speed.

"So what's in it?" Robert screamed.

"DOREEN," Larry shouted down the track.

"DOREEN FOREVER!"

"THE SEVEN STARS ARE THE ANGELS OF THE SEVEN CHURCHES — AND THE SEVEN CANDLESTICKS WHICH THOU SAWEST ARE THE SEVEN CHURCHES . . . "

This is going to take forever, thought Robert. Why can't he just tell me all that stuff like before. Why do I have to read it out loud?

And why seven everything, he thought. Why not seven hundred? Or seven thousand?

Every night his grandfather made him read to him in bed. Most of the stuff he had to read was about money — like the stock-market report. But now he had to read from the *Book of Revelations.*

I got it really good when he just told me — like the serpent ripping into pieces and spiralling down into a bottomless pit and the false prophet and the battle with the beast. That was a good bit. And Alpha and Omega — the beginning and the end. Those guys are great! But "sawest" this and "sawest" that? Reading just makes it boring.

Boring boring boring. Seven churches — seven stars — seven angels go to Mars.

"Why do you want me to read this stuff when you don't even like churches, Grandpa?"

"'Cause there's things to learn from it — that's why."

"Like what?"

"I'm not tellin' ya."

"Why not?"

"'Cause you gotta learn for yourself. Ya gotta read the words so you can figure out the signs."

"Why don't you just tell me the signs like before?"

"Because you gotta learn to look for yourself."

"But I liked it better when you told me."

"You don't want anyone tellin' ya nothing Robert."

"I liked you telling me about the guy coming outta the east and fighting and the two-edged sword and the horses of fire. Tell me the bit about wars and rumours of wars."

"Read it yourself."

"Danny's dad reads him the Hardy Boy books."

"Well hardy-har for Danny's dad!"

"Hardy what?"

"Hardy-har!"

"For who?"

"For Danny's dad."

"Oh."

They both lay quietly for a moment. Then his grandfather spoke.

"You finish *Revelations* and I'll get ya somethin' else from the library. Maybe *Moby Dick* — or T. S. Elliot. Or maybe this Italian fella who wrote *The Divine Comedy*."

"Yeah — let's get the comedy one. I want something funny. Is it really funny?"

"Breaks me up every time."

"Let's get it!"

"If that goddamn Mrs. Beatty can find it. Told me last week she didn't know if the bible was in circulation and what was I doin' with a library card anyway seein' as I was blind. I said it was a bestseller so it sure as hell better be in circulation 'cause I need the damn thing to prop up my wheelbarrow. And you get on with finishing *Revelations* Robert. I ain't paying that bitch no late fine for a goddamn bible . . . "

"What about the Italian guy?"

"Dante?"

"Did he write lots of funny stuff?"

"Dante wrote about great battles."

"Funny battles?"

"He wrote about heaven and hell. And the universe — flyin' around up there like nobody's business."

"And all the stars bashing into each other and stuff, right?"

"The heavens whirl around us, he said — in all their glory. That's what this fellah said — glory. And still mans' eyes are cast upon the ground."

"What does that mean?"

"He was telling ya to look up. Get your heads outta your asses and look, he said. The sky goes on forever — you're part of it. You're a tiny part of infinity!"

Robert's grandfather was always talking about infinity.

"And when ya know that Robert, then anything is possible."

"But then this Italian guy wrote *The Divine Comedy*, right Grandpa?"

"After he wrote the Hardy Boy Series."

"Did he?"

"When are you going to stop believing what people tell ya, Robert?"

"Tomorrow. I'll stop believing what people tell me tomorrow, okay Grandpa?"

"Okay."

He reached over and turned off the light because his grandfather always forgot.

"There's signs up there, Robert. You gotta look up . . . "

His grandfather wouldn't stop talking.

" . . . into the eternal darkness, into fire and into ice."

So he rolled into the darkness and tried to sleep.

"Their sighs, lamentations and loud wailing resounded through the starless air, so that at first it made me weep . . . whirling through the air forever dark . . . "

Every afternoon after lunch, Robert sat at the kitchen table and watched his grandfather take a jackknife from the back pocket of his overalls. He'd cut an apple into wedges and a hunk of cheese into thin slices. Then he'd throw salt over the table hoping some of it would land on the pieces of apple. Robert always closed his eyes in case his grandpa missed. He didn't mind salt in his hair. Just not in his eyes. When the first piece of cheese and apple went into his grandpa's mouth to start the slow chew, he knew it was time to read him *Alley Oop* from the funny papers.

Today he couldn't get on with his reading because his grandmother was talking too much. So he watched the huge Adam's apple wobbling up and down in the old-man throat. Chew — wobble wobble. Just like a turkey, Robert thought. Chew — wobble wobble. Chew.

"Go or don't go. It's no skin off my back," said Flo. "I know ya got a letter. Angus down at the post office says ya got a letter. And they sent one to the doctor too, tellin' him it was all arranged."

Will Coutts ignored his wife and carried on with the business at hand. Chew — wobble wobble. Chew — wobble wobble.

"But I'll tell ya one thing — if ya don't go I don't want no whinin' about not bein' able to see. This is your last chance Will. If ya don't get on that train you'll stay blind as a bat for the rest of your pathetic goddamn life."

Robert thought his granny was getting mean. He'd never heard his grandpa whine in his pathetic goddamn life even once.

Chew — wobble wobble. Chew.

"If I had my say I'd just have ya put down and that'd be the end of it. Pile up all that eye lotion junk that don't do ya no good anyways — start a bonfire. Then I'd bring in the neighbours and have a hell of a party!"

Robert figured his granny was grumpy and just wanted to have an argument, because he knew there wasn't any letter. He was the expert on letters. That was his job. If there was a letter he'd have read it to his grandpa in their bedroom before lunch. That's why his grandpa made him learn to read in the first place, so his granny never got to know anything — like about stocks and bonds and stuff.

"Probably better for your health if you can't see anyway ya old bugger. Don't wanna have a heart attack when ya look in the mirror." Flo slammed the dishes into the kitchen sink.

This is great, thought Robert. If she keeps talking maybe I won't have to go to school at all. He was usually late for school in the afternoon anyway. His teacher got used to it. She knew he couldn't leave until he'd finished *Alley Oop*. Besides, she was too afraid of Will Coutts to cause a fuss.

"It's scaring the children concerns me Will, walking all over town with that one eye floatin' all over the place."

Chew — wobble wobble.

If his grandfather was eating an orange, Robert wondered, would it be called an Adam's orange?

"So if ya decide to be blind the rest of your life, do us a favour ya scary bastard. Head down to the Co-op and get yourself a paper bag to stick over your head. Let the little darlin's get a good night's sleep for a change."

Boy is she cranky, thought Robert. Usually she left them alone to read the funnies, but today she stayed in the kitchen to bang dishes.

Robert started to think about the route he'd take home from school just in case he had to go. Problem was there were only so many new routes you could take home from anywhere in Biggar.

Every afternoon after school, Russell Matthews and his brothers waited for him so they could kill him. They'd chase him until he got to his front door.

Running down Main Street was always a pretty good bet because he could deke into the Five and Dime. He just wished that Rita woman who worked there would stop ruffling up his hair. Ever since all that salt flew out of his head and landed in the comic books because his grandfather missed the apple big-time, that Rita woman kept ruffling up his hair. She'd laugh and say she was looking for pepper or something dumb.

Maybe today I'll try running through Mrs. Curry's yard and then up the back alley, he thought.

Chew — wobble wobble. Chew.

Or maybe I should just take a kitchen knife and let them have it in front of the firehall.

Russell and his family were out for revenge. Robert'd knocked out Russell's new front tooth with a baseball bat and his mum was really mad. They were the poor kids living on social assistance at the end of town and his mum couldn't afford to get any new teeth.

"So do what you want Will, but this is your last chance."

Will Coutts wiped the apple juice off his jackknife and folded it into his overalls.

Flo stomped off to the front bedroom for her afternoon nap. She sat on her bed and fumed. Why can't he just get on the bloody train? It's a cataract for Pete's sake — they yank 'em off all the time down there.

She heaved out a sigh. She knew she was wasting her breath. He didn't go last time; he probably won't go now.

Robert opened the newspaper to the funnies. Alley Oop was in a jungle tree pulling at a vine and talking to the dinosaur below.

He read: "THESE VINES ARE JUST THE THING TO MAKE A SWELL ANIMAL TRAP! YEZZIR, DINNY, OL' PAL — YOU'RE GONNA GET A BIG SURPRISE WHEN YA SEE WHAT OL' ALLEY IS GONNA DO WITH THESE!"

That was pretty simple, thought Robert. A lot easier than the *Book of Revelations*. Then he explained what he saw in the next three boxes. There were no words. Just a WHUMP and an ARGHHHHHHH.

"Dinny yanks down on the vine and Ol' Alley falls right outta the tree and crashes — WHUMP! Then Alley has stars coming out of his head. So he picks up his axe and chases Dinny right out of the forest — ARGHHHHHHH!"

Robert waited for his grandpa to say something. "How come you didn't laugh, Grandpa?"

Will Coutts got up to go into the bedroom.

"Maybe if you went to get your eye fixed you could see the pictures and see how funny it is," Robert yelled after him.

Will Coutts turned around in the doorframe. "Don't you start too. Go to school — you're gonna be late."

"I'm always late."

"Good boy. Keep it up," and he disappeared into the bedroom.

That night, Robert finished another chapter from the *Book of Revelations*. He'd had lots of trouble with the "holdeths" and the "haths." It made him mad as hell. And he was already mad enough at his grandpa.

"So how come you like the bible and stuff but we don't go to church?" he asked.

"I don't like the bible."

"Yes you do."

"I like the *Book of Revelations.*"

"But how come we don't go to church?"

"'Cause it's full of people who are too goddamn scared to see what's starin' em straight in their goddamn face."

"You're scared to see!"

Robert held his breath. He knew his grandpa must have got a letter from the doctors and didn't even let him read it. He was really mad — it's okay to read *Revelations* but it's not okay to read a letter!

Will Coutts turned over on the bed and yanked the covers up. Robert reached over his grandfather's large body and turned off the light.

He always forgets to pull the switch, grumbled Robert. Not everyone's blind you know. He should just go get his eye fixed, then he could read for himself and I could sleep.

Robert listened to old-man sounds coming from the ancient body next to him and smelled the mustiness of the bedclothes. What's he so scared of anyway? Why's he so scared of seeing?

I got more to be scared of than him — I got the Russell Gang on my tail.

He remembered the close call he had that afternoon and decided he'd better think up a new route home for tomorrow. Then he heard his grandfather breathe deeply and roll over onto his back. He knew he was going to tell him stuff.

"What do ya see out the window, Robert?"

"I see stars, Grandpa."

"Yes — stars. And you know that past those stars are more stars. It goes on forever. There's no concrete block at the end of the universe — just forever."

Robert looked past the plastic curtains into the night. He knew there was more to come.

"And inside your head there's just as many stars. But we forget to look. Just like we forget to look up, we forget to look in. Inside my head I see those stars. I don't need to look out your goddamn window."

His grandfather's voice sounded angry.

"So don't you go tellin' me I should get my eye fixed, Robert. Or I gotta even look with my eyes. I'll see the universe any goddamn way I want. We all march to a different beat."

Here we go again, thought Robert. March — march. Beat — beat.

"It ain't none of your business how I see things."

"But the universe goes on forever Grandpa. You gotta look past the concrete block. For infinity and all that."

"You're damn right you gotta! But you can listen too. You can close your eyes and listen. You can hear the universe. Feel it. It's on the inside too."

"But you can't see me."

"Yes I can. And it's not up to you to tell me what I see and what I can't see. It not your business. Or your granny's business. It's my business."

"I'm going to close my eyes for a whole day so I can see what you see, Grandpa."

"Like hell you are!"

Robert's head was starting to pound. "Nobody can see what somebody else sees. You gotta look for yourself, and never believe what you see the first time. You gotta look twice."

"Okay, Grandpa."

"Anything is possible. There's a whole goddamn universe out there for chrissake — there's things ya can't even imagine. But you gotta keep your eyes wide open. Look for the signs. Your signs — nobody else's. And not just with your eyes — listen for 'em."

"Okay, Grandpa."

"The world's changin' — nothin' will be the same when you grow up. And ya gotta be ready. There'll be earthquakes and wars and rumours of wars . . . "

Robert closed his eyes as tightly as he could. Red and white dots floated inside his head. He thought he could see the beast opening the heavens with its sword of fire.

The next day Robert sat trying to finish his rice pudding. His grandfather was wearing a white starched shirt. There was a suitcase packed at his feet. His granny was clearing up the dishes from lunch.

He was too worried to ask his grandpa why he changed his mind about catching the train. He asked him what he should do about the Russell Gang instead.

"Stop runnin'," said his grandfather.

161

"But they'll pound me."

"Surprise 'em."

"How?"

"Stop runnin'. Turn right around — make your face look scary as hell — and start chasing them."

"How do I make my face scary?"

"Ask your granny — seems to work for me."

"Granny?"

"Imagine the Dow Jones average crashed," replied Flo. "Then pull your lip up over your head like you're gonna scream and pop your eyes out. You'll look just like the scary bastard sittin' across from ya."

Robert's granny laughed from all the way down in her belly.

"What'll they do then Grandpa?"

"They'll be so goddamn surprised they'll turn on their tails and take off into oblivion."

"Ya — once they pound the shit outta ya," warned his grandma.

Robert started to worry again.

Flo folded her apron. Then she left the kitchen to go for her nap.

"Good luck, Will," she said.

Will Coutts got out his jackknife and Robert opened the funnies to *Alley Oop*.

Robert ran into the house and through to the back room. He had a bloody nose, his elbows were skinned, and his grandpa was gone. Oh great, he thought. What a stupid time to get his stupid goddamn eye fixed. He lay down on the bed to stop the blood from pouring into his mouth.

When he'd come out of school, they were waiting — all
four of them. Russell was whistling and spitting through the
gap in his front teeth. Whistle and spit. Whistle and spit. His
brothers were flexing their muscles like they thought they
were in some kind of motorcycle gang or something.

Robert shot off like a bat out of hell around the back of
the school, straight through a grade-four girls' soccer game,
and then back into the building and out the front door again
thinking he could lose them in a route of stupidity. But the
Russell Gang were right on his tail.

So he took off as fast as he could over to Main Street,
speeding past the firehall, the movie theatre, the bakery and
making pretty good time to the Five and Dime. But they were
getting closer. He could feel hot breath wheezing through
the gap in Russell's front teeth.

Then a picture of that Rita woman popped into his head.
"Rita," his brain kept saying. "Rita — Rita — Rita." His body
sped up even faster as he listened to the inside of his head.
He could only think of Rita.

"Rita, Rita — Ruffle my hair . . . Rita, Rita — Ruffle it
good . . . Rita, Rita — Ruffle my hair . . . Rita, Rita — Ruffle
it . . . "

Just as he was heading into the store's front door, his
grandfather's voice took over on the inside of his brain. "Stop
running," it said. "Stop."

Robert squealed to a halt in front of the Five and Dime,
catching a glimpse of the Rita woman standing close to the
window. He'd stopped running. He'd stopped!

Then he heard his grandfather's voice again. "Turn around
Robert," it said.

So he spun around to face the Gang. They were about
five feet back. They'd stopped too. They were looking at him

suspicious like, as if they wanted to pounce but were making sure he didn't have a secret weapon like a knife.

It's working, Robert thought. It's goddamn working.

"Now make your face scary as hell."

Robert opened his mouth and pulled his upper lip back over his front teeth. Then he raised his eyebrows and stretched his forehead muscles back to the unchartered regions of his scull. Finally he poked his eyes out as far as they could poke.

The gang stepped back in amazement.

Then Alley Oop took over on the inside of his head. "You're going to get a big surprise Russell Ol' pal when ya see what Ol' Alley and Ol' Robert are gonna do to you and your dinny-dinks!"

Robert walked towards the enemy.

The Russell Gang laughed so hard they could hardly keep their swings straight. Still, they managed to knee him in the stomach, kick him in the side, and push him over so his elbows ploughed into the pavement. When he looked up, Russell landed him a whopper right on the nose.

Rita came out of the Five and Dime and yelled at them to clear out. She told Robert to come in the store so she could get something for his nose but Robert took off in the other direction. He circled around through back alleys so nobody would see him getting home.

Last time I'll ever listen to my grandpa, decided Robert.

Flo stood at the bedroom door. "Well at least ya still got your front teeth, Sunshine," she said.

"Did Grandpa get to Rochester?"

"No."

"Did he get to Saskatoon?"

"No."

"Where'd he get?"

"He got to the beer parlour."

Robert saw how hard his granny was chewing the left side of her lip. "He'll go next time Granny."

"No he won't. Come in the kitchen — let me fix that nose."

After supper, Flo went over to Mrs. Potts' to read her cards. Robert sat and waited until it started to get dark. He didn't want anyone to see his smashed-up nose. Then he walked down the railroad tracks and cut over to the beer parlour.

Sitting out front was his grandpa's wheelbarrow. It was holding the suitcase. Robert took it out and climbed in. He waited.

Men staggered out every once in a while and looked at the boy in the wheelbarrow. They left him alone because they knew he was Will Coutts' grandchild.

Robert felt good. He liked the smell of smoke from the room behind him and the sound of men's laughter and the clinking of glasses. I can hardly wait till I can be a beer-parlour man, the boy thought.

He looked across to the train station and then over above the grain elevator. It was a beautiful night. The stars were just out. The wind was warm. Summer was coming.

He felt safe. He figured the Russell Gang were all piled into their one bed listening to that stupid whistling sound coming from the gap in Russell's teeth. He hoped they lived on assistance forever and had to eat fried leftover porridge for supper.

He looked again above the grain elevator and saw the Big Dipper. He counted the stars. Seven . . . seven bright stars. Why seven, he wondered. Are those the seven candles? Or maybe the angels? He tried to look beyond them to see if he could find the beast.

He thought about his grandfather looking at the universe. Looking out there any goddamn way he wanted. He thought about being blind. About listening. It's his business, decided Robert. He chose to be blind. He likes looking in. I just hope he knows he'll be blind forever. And that means forever. Forever and ever.

I like looking out, he thought. Past the stars. Past infinity.

The sky seemed to grow larger.

The darkness began to fill with light. Robert decided to keep his eyes open without blinking.

I can see the universe any way I want, he thought. Seven candles — seven stars — seven angels go to Mars.

He looked over again at the grain elevator. It looked like it was falling, the way a tree looks when you stare too long at the top branch. He felt a bit dizzy and turned away. You gotta look twice, he heard his grandfather say.

Yes — the grain elevator was falling. Very slowly. It began to lean towards him. Robert didn't feel like being afraid. It was falling too gently.

Anything is possible, his grandpa said. There are things in this world you can't even imagine.

Robert wanted to see them. He wanted to see. He wanted to see past the concrete block. He wanted to see the beast. The signs in the sky. Earthquakes and wars and rumours of wars.

Infinity. He wanted to go past infinity.

He kept his eyes wide open.

The grain elevator bowed forward and lifted off the ground. It fell through itself and rose into a full circle in the air. The stars moved in streams of colour. The sky was full of signs.

Robert thought he could hear a rumbling coming from far off in the galaxy . . . an earthquake . . . or a white horse thundering towards the beast. The sky blazed with streaks of light. Meteors flashed signals to earth. Planets. Glowing shadows. Explosions of fire.

Any way I want, he thought.

He heard a strange whistling sound coming from a cluster of stars. He looked twice to figure out what it was. The stars looked like the front row of somebody's teeth. Then he saw a hole. Like a gap. And it got bigger. And bigger. A spray of star-bullets splashed out the gap and whistled through space.

It was the Russell gang! And they were riding with the Hardy Boys! It was a shoot-out in the universe. They were blasting their death-rays into the hide-out galaxies of the beast.

The heavens whirled above in all their glory.

Pow! Pow! Robert heard a huge scream and saw shiny white specks sparkling all over the universe. Russell had crashed straight into one of the Hardy Boys and smashed out the rest of his teeth. They twinkled in the darkness. Blood gushed out of his nose.

It's the Divine Comedy, Robert thought. I'm in the Divine Comedy!

He saw light galloping into the empty black. Leaping and swirling onto jungle vines — ropes of glimmering hair swaying high in the star dust. "Rita. Rita. Rita."

He saw gigantic dinosaurs running for their lives, star-salt spraying into the distant caves of infinity, and heard a WHUMP so loud streams of comets poured out of Alley Oop's head. "ARGHHHHHHHHHH!"

Then he saw his own face floating over the moon. It was horrible — the skin stretched so far back it looked like it was ready to snap off his head. WHAAAPPPPP! The face whizzed through space like a crazy balloon. It was so goddamn scary even all hell turned on its tail and started to run. "Rita. Rita. Rita." "Rita. Rita. Rita."

Suddenly the sky shot purple and red. Hot lava spilled from the tops of mountains.

Robert heard the voice of the trumpet.

It's Revelations, he panicked. I'm in the Revelations!

The heavens whirled. The sky turned scary.

Black smoke floated in from all the corners of the universe. Stars began to fall towards Earth. A lake of flames filled up the sky — and out of the fire crawled the beast. It had seven-hundred heads and seven-thousand mouths.

Robert was frightened. He wanted to close his eyes.

Then he heard the rumbling again. Like thunder racing across the sky. When he looked past the lake of flames, he thought he could see a horse. Galloping. Galloping towards the beast.

And on the horse's back was a warrior. And behind them both was an army. Chasing the warrior with spears of fire.

Flames zoomed across the heavens.

The warrior opened his mouth and started spinning his head. Knives shot out of his throat. Seven-million knives. The army screamed and howled. Arms and legs splashed blood all over space. The horse kicked up his legs and stamped at the flying heads.

Then one of the warrior's eyes caught on fire. And when he stopped spinning his head to see what was going on — the eye flew out of his head. Just like a bird. It flew into the air like a burning bird. And when the warrior tried to grab the eye, the army ambushed him and threw him into the burning lake. Seven-thousand mouths reached out of the fire and brimstone.

Suddenly a light flashed in the sky. And out of the light — seven angels flew toward the beast, their wings flapping to the edges of infinity. They flapped and flapped and made such a huge noise the army ran for its life.

When the angels got to the beast, they wrapped it in a chain and heaved it into a bottomless pit.

The fire died. The stars floated back into the heavens and curled around the dead eye. They carried it to eternity. The man on the horse was gone. The battle was over.

I am Alpha and I am Omega, Robert heard his head say to him. I am the beginning and the end.

Robert's head felt very large. And his eyes hurt. He looked down at his scrunched-up knees in the wheelbarrow. He didn't want to look up anymore. He just wanted to look at his knees.

He knew he should be figuring out his signs but he was too tired. Tomorrow — he'd think about them tomorrow. Anyway, he was only a tiny part of infinity.

He wanted to close his eyes but was afraid of what he might see on the inside. So he listened to the sound of a steam engine pulling out of the railway station.

If I was blind I'd wear a really great patch, he thought. Like a pirate or a motorcycle guy. A black patch — or maybe yellow. I'd paint snakes on it. Or an eye. Yeah — an eye. Or maybe seven eyes. Yeah — seven. I'd paint seven eyes. Seven candles — seven stars — seven angels go to Mars.

He fell asleep.

Finally, he felt his grandfather's hand on his back.

He got out of the wheelbarrow and picked up the suitcase. They started to walk home along the railroad tracks.

Robert liked the crunching sound of gravel that the wheelbarrow made beside the tracks. He hadn't heard it since last summer. He looked at the black steel rails catching the reflection of the sky.

Maybe I should ask Russell if he wants to play with me and Danny tomorrow, he thought. We could play cops and robbers. Or Alley Oop? Or maybe we could play Armageddon.

The old man stopped. Robert looked up at him.

"The heavens are whirling, Grandpa," said the boy.

"I know," replied Will Coutts.

"How do you know?"

"It's the Northern Lights."

"But how do you know?"

"I can hear them."

The Day the Queen Came to Town

Part One

"I hear the ol' dear walked into her living room and there was her little bow-wow," said Mrs. Baker to her neighbour, "all dressed up in that cute fuzzy overcoat, stiff as a board, his doggy body twisted up grotesque all over the linoleum floor, and his little doggy paws reaching under the door like he was tryin' to get out or somethin' unnatural."

"A pity," replied Mrs. Perkins. "I swear it took the poor old dear all winter to knit that coat."

"Never thought that animal would finally kick the bucket. And back on Valentines Day to boot!"

For the first time in over twenty years, Mrs. Jenkins walked out of her front door on the first day of spring without her beloved Pekinese. Mr. Switzer, the undertaker, was standing on his veranda when he saw her coming down the street. "One down and one to go!" he gloated.

The winter had been a good one for Mrs. Curry over on Fourth Avenue. She came out onto her front porch as senile as ever. Eric Meisner, the bingo caller, suggested the community do something special for her seeing as she was going to be a hundred in July.

People all over town were in their yards talking to neighbours, trying to catch up on the gossip they might have missed during their long hibernation.

"I hear they might be letting Gladys Potts' niece out of the loony bin in North Battleford," continued Mrs. Baker.

"Imagine trying to drown yourself in a wringer-washing machine."

"Well they say cleanliness is next to godliness."

"And I don't blame the Finlaysons going to the school board saying they don't want any shenanigans going on in their barn this graduation night — last graduation their daughter Melanie got pregnant twice."

"You can't get pregnant twice."

"They don't know if it was the Hodgenson boy or that party-crasher from Perdue. Baby's as cute as a button though."

The town was abuzz with news that a team of researchers from the university in Saskatoon were to spend the summer in Biggar following the Baily Twins around and putting wires on their heads.

Apparently early one January morning, Sam started speaking in tongues and at exactly the same time his brother Orvil threw his head back and screamed, "He's under the tractor with Jesus!" Mrs. Baily ran to the barn to find her husband pinned under the John Deer, and from that time on speaking in tongues with simultaneous translation became a daily occurrence. Mr. and Mrs. Baily got so fed up they called the university and asked for a cure.

Robert's life was in turmoil that spring. His Aunt Doreen and her two kids had run away from the tattooed man and moved lock, stock and barrel into his house. His granny made a bedroom in the back hallway for his cousins, and their mother slept on the veranda. The girl was okay when she wasn't whining for her daddy, but Daren was a nuisance. He kept smashing things. Not always on purpose. Things just got bust wherever he went. Like his grandpa's radio and his grandma's ironing board and the E below middle C on the piano. It was boring having to hide all your stuff all the time so your dumb cousin couldn't wreck it.

At least the swimming pool will be open last week in June, thought Robert. There's that to look forward to. Maybe my cousin'll drown.

In early May the news hit town like a hurricane. The Queen was coming! Elizabeth herself — Queen of England — was on her way to Biggar!

Not since 1939, when the Queen Mother toured the provinces, had royalty visited the small prairie town. Now after nearly two decades it was happening again. Only this time it was the lovely "new" Queen — one minute in Africa playing dolls in her treehouse, and now Queen of the entire Commonwealth of Nations!

She was to arrive by locomotive.

Near the end of June, late in the day, a Royal Coach would be pulling up to the CNR station. The Queen was to descend onto the train platform, walk across to a limousine — "open top for sure," said the mayor — and roll up one side of the street and down the other. "All part of a national plan," added the mayor. "She's rolling up and down Main Streets all across the country."

Once Her Highness got back on board, she'd only be travelling a few miles further west. The steam engine was meant to switch tracks and puff over to a siding by some trees, where the Queen would sleep for the night with her husband, Prince Phillip.

"There's a hell of a good clump of trees just a couple of minutes out of town," pointed out the mayor. "Ideal for sleeping."

Town Council asked Eric Meisner, a splendid volunteer for community events as well as a darn good bingo-caller, to set up a committee to guarantee that this stop on the Royal Journey would do the town proud. The first idea that popped into Eric's head was to present Mrs. Curry to the Queen as the oldest person in Biggar. The mayor said he wasn't keen on the idea because the old dear had been senile for years and might think Her Majesty was the railway conductor.

Eric set up committee meetings pretty well every night. Gladys Potts volunteered to do the minutes with the hope he might make a mess of it so she could slip up the ranks and take over the whole kit and caboodle. This was not an opportunity Gladys was going to waste. She was a true resource person when it came to matters of the royalty and always prided herself on being a monarchist. She'd hung a Union Jack in her front window for as long as she could remember.

The committee went into action. Decorations were ordered for the event, repair work proceeded on sidewalks and public buildings, and security issues were a top priority with the local RCMP. Harold Struthers, vice-chair of the committee and head of the school board, ordered the high-school band and glee club to start polishing up "God Save the Queen". He also announced an essay contest about Saskatchewan's role in the Commonwealth, open only to students with an above D average, which pretty well left out all the kids on the east side. The mayor agreed the winner could stand with the welcoming committee and give the essay to the Queen. It was also decided to postpone the opening of the swimming pool until the Royal Visit was over. With all the work to be done, town council couldn't afford the manpower to get it ready.

Robert and his friends hated the damn Queen and her whole Royal Family.

As summer approached, the committee began to worry about the weather. All signs pointed to another dry, squint-eyed, dust-in-your-mouth summer like last year. And what about the slough? With all that heat, it smelled to high heaven. And the mosquitoes? Not to mention the grasshoppers. What about the grasshoppers?

Some of the old-timers said it was all horseshit; if she didn't like the place she could turn around and go back to where she came from.

When the committee went to visit Will Coutts to suggest he invest in some paint and do something about the eyesores he owned along Main Street, he told the buggers he didn't believe in the Royal Family. He was a Trotskyist way back near the turn of the century and ever since then he knew monarchy was the root of all evil — as far as he was concerned it was business as usual. If he wanted to walk up Main Street on the day of the "phoo-for-all" he'd walk up Main Street — and if any damn Queen was driving by in her Royal Jalopy he'd dent her in the Royal Fender with his Royal Wheelbarrow!

"Better than doing his exercises in his all together with his you-know-what flappin' in the air outside a certain designated clump of trees," informed Mr. Meisner, looking on the bright side.

Only Mrs. Potts recognized the severity of the problem. She went over to the library to look up "Trotskyist" and was alarmed at her discovery. Even though Will Coutts didn't go to church, she'd always assumed that somewhere deep down he was a Christian. After all, he fed that strange grandson of his all that scary stuff from the *Book of Revelations*. But this Trotsky fellow was no God-fearing man that was for darn sure. He was part of that gang that did in the Tsar and even Anastasia for crying out loud.

Gladys marched over to the mayor's office with this piece of news added to her list of concerns.

"First — the slough. What are you going to do about it? And then there's the matter of the curtsey. Do you and your honourable wives have the least idea of the importance of the curtsey? There can be no movement in the upper areas of the spine when you do the dip. I'm prepared to offer tuition if you like. I'll even stand right along on the platform."

The mayor told Mrs. Potts he had everything under control and that his wife was a grand curtsier, but thank you very much. The general opinion around town was that Gladys wasn't firing on all cylinders since her niece was taken away, so he wanted to be respectful.

"And what about security? I just got back from trying to talk some reason into that old Will Coutts — the naked blind half-wit with all that money who does any fool thing that comes into his mind? Did you know the old lunatic's a communist? Studied with Trotsky I understand. I know his wife — she's got a cross to bear I can tell you. Now this Trotsky believed in revolution — he and his cohorts shot their king. I'm not saying Mr. Coutts is about to blow up the Royal Coach — he is blind after all — but I did hear him say in a public gathering that the monarchy is the root of all evil, so he's already causing mischief!"

Gladys took a breath.

"I think it would behove you well, your worship, to place the old scoundrel under arrest for the day. If he's not out there causing a disturbance for the crowd, I guarantee he'll be swinging his member out in a wheatfield close enough to the encampment to cause a disturbance for the Queen. Besides, he won't lift a paint brush to those slum buildings he owns across from the Five and Dime."

When the widow woman finally left, the mayor called his wife to suggest she start practising the curtsey.

Flo Coutts was furious when she heard what Gladys was up to. She stomped right over and gave her old friend a piece of her mind. "If he's a commie that's between him and the big fellah — not nobody else. And if you and your goddamn committee are so concerned about the old man bein' around on the day of the Queen, just give him a bottle of sherry and send him over to Erica Olsen at the hotel."

Flo'd had it with Gladys, and besides, ever since her daughter got a job she was too busy taking care of the grandchildren to spend time with the silly bitch anyway.

Early in June, Doreen started working in an office down at the Wheat Pool. Robert's grandmother told him he'd have to watch Daren more and take him along when he went out to play. "And don't make a fuss," she told him. "Everyone has to pull their weight around here." Oh great, thought Robert, there goes Danny's new baseball bat. Daren will bust it for sure.

Doreen was relieved to hear that her husband was arrested for trying to rob the Army and Navy Store back in Edmonton. She didn't have the heart to tell her kids yet, but at least could stop worrying about him coming around the corner any minute. She even started to have a bit of fun. The night her mother sent her to the movies she met this guy who sold the popcorn at the confectionary. He used to be a Mountie but got fed up and quit — said he wanted to be a writer. She had coffee with him a couple of times down at the café during her lunch break and even met him once after work. Doreen couldn't figure out if he'd written anything yet.

On the first of December last year, Constable Schumacher bit the bullet and quit the force. From the moment he took the call and discovered Edna Potts' naked body flopping like a fish on her aunt's basement steps, he knew he had to be a writer.

For six months he worked part-time at the newspaper and the movie theatre, returning late at night to his cold little apartment above the drugstore to write poetry. He wanted to lay down words — images — a tribute to the enchanted sea creature who'd inspired him so deeply. He sat wrapped in his Hudson's Bay blanket like a predatory bird ready to strike its prey the moment the muse entered the room, his arm aching from the sharp pencil he held taut above his notebook. But for six months nothing happened. He could not force the weapon of his creativity to the lined white target below.

Then he met Doreen down at the theatre — Will Coutts' daughter. That night he went home, picked up his pencil, and filled his entire notebook. He wrote about fish: sturgeon, trout, plaice, salmon, herring, pickerel, mackerel, barracuda and cod.

Midway through June, Alister was sitting in his apartment still writing about fish when Gladys Potts paid him a late-night visit. The moon leaked through Schumacher's one tiny window onto the woman's pale oval face.

"I need your help," whispered the distressed widow.

Alister put down his pencil. "What can I do for you, Mrs. Potts?"

"It's about Will Coutts. Ever since you arrested him for parading around naked in the Finlayson's wheatfield you're the only one who can handle him."

Alister was struck with the tone of her sincerity.

"Get on with it Potts."

"He's a Red, Mr. Schumacher. And nobody's willing to do a blessed thing about it. I thought I could handle it alone, but I can't. I've been to the committee, the mayor, the RCMP. He's going to cause trouble, I can feel it; they're programmed to cause trouble. Our Monarch could die, Mr. Schumacher — if not of physical injury, certainly of embarrassment. You have to keep him away Sir."

Alister had no problem with the request. It gave him a chance to get on the good side of Doreen's father. And he might even have the nerve to tell the old guy he was finally writing.

"Don't worry," he assured the over-wrought widow woman. "It'll be my pleasure."

Then he returned to his poem. "Sword-fish, jelly-fish, gold-fish fly . . . angel-fish soar in a sun-fish sky."

PART TWO

It was a week before the event and Eric Meisner was in a frenzy of confusion. None of the little union jacks on sticks had arrived from the East, the parents of the student who won the essay contest were insisting she get to read it out loud on the platform, there were no less than a dozen reports of slough-smell, Will Coutts' block along Main Street still looked like shit, and half the high-school glee club who fell out of

Finlayson's hayloft during graduation were still being treated for concussion.

The only certainty in the whole affair was the order of key events. When the Royal Coach pulled into the station, Biggar children, handpicked from Sunday-school congregations around town, were to cheer and wave their little union jacks on a stick, if the goddamn things ever arrived, as the school band and glee club performed "God Save the Queen". Then the welcoming committee was to present her with flowers, a framed photograph of her mother standing on the same platform during the dirty thirties, and the essay.

There would be handshaking — women in white gloves — and the curtseys. Only town council, their wives, the girl with the essay, and a few prominent Biggar businessmen were allowed on the welcoming stand. Eric Meisner tried his darnedest to get old Mrs. Curry up there for presentation but the mayor was adamantly opposed. Called it a security issue. The only exception was an Indian Chief being shipped in from a reserve north of Prince Albert. Rumour had it the Queen herself made the request through the use of CNR telegraph services.

The Royal Party were then to step into the open car and drive all the way up one side of Main Street to the highway, execute a wide U-turn by the hospital, where she could wave to the sick, and return down the other side. There was to be no stopping however — a protocol official made that absolutely clear.

Then onto the train — fond farewells from the caboose — and five miles to the designated rest area where she would spend the evening with her husband, Prince Phillip.

Eric was beginning to hope the darn thing would just get itself over with. The weather continued to be hot and dry as the big day grew closer. No relief in sight. The hardware ran out of mosquito spray and the grasshoppers finished with outlying areas, so they started in on the town.

Alister checked in everyday on Gladys Potts to assure her that he'd take care of the old man on the day of the event. The woman was very tense and it was all she could do to keep her hands from shaking as she gave him progress reports on the long purple outfit she was sewing to wear for the Queen. It couldn't be described as a dress exactly. It was more regal. She was also pinning together strips of red, white and blue chiffon to construct a hat to resemble a Union Jack. Gladys looked forward to the visits from her young champion and only wished she was a few years younger herself.

Entering Mrs. Potts' house always made Alister feel a bit flushed. He'd never forget the water pouring onto the cellar floor — soapsuds, cardboard boxes, crayons bobbing over the surface of the flood — and the unfortunate Edna Potts almost dead after trying to drown herself in her aunt's second-hand wringer washing machine. It was exotic. Disturbing. Wet. And he still adored his creature of the sea.

Rumour had it that Edna was doing very well with her recuperation in the mental institution up in North Battleford. Rumour also had it she and the man who tried to break through the cellar window were to be married. Ah well, Alister would sigh. Perhaps there's Doreen. Even though he knew she could never bark like a seal.

Robert and his best friend Danny became more and more resentful about the delay of the pool's opening. Two days before the stupid Queen was supposed to come, Danny's little brother caught up with Robert and Danny down at the fair-grounds. He could hardly get the words out he was so excited.

What the two boys understood from Danny's brother was that some kid called Luke just talked to his dad who just got back from Saskatoon who heard the news from some guy in a barbershop. Biggar was gonna be full of crooks! Everyone was going downtown to wave flags everywhere, so these robbers were following the Queen all across Canada, and when everyone did their stupid waving stuff, these robbers just walked into people's houses with their sacks and helped themselves.

Danny told his brother he was dumb, but he and Robert hid their bikes just to be safe. Daren watched with alarm.

The next day, Daren walked out of his house with his pockets full of pennies — just in case any of the crooks arrived early — but the pennies were so heavy they pulled his pants down. When he bent over to pull them up, he fell into a bush and crashed into Danny's bike.

"Oh great," hollered Danny. "First my new baseball bat and now my new bike!"

Danny told Robert he was fed up with all the Coutts' and wasn't gonna stand on the same side of the street tomorrow with any of them. Robert seriously considered becoming a Trotskyist like his grandfather.

When Alister Schumacher dropped into the house that night, Doreen was hoping he might ask her if she wanted to stand along Main Street with him. Instead, he asked her father if he wanted to get out of town tomorrow. He wasn't planning to stick around for the Queen and was going for a walk in the country. Doreen was a bit taken aback but was beginning to get used to his peculiarities. Anyway, she thought to herself, I really should be with the kids.

Will said he was planning to get as far away from the goddamn royal bullshit as he could. He was headin' outta town before noon and if Schumacher wanted to tag along that was his own goddamn business.

PART THREE

The morning finally arrived. Robert's granny was really cranky. She kept saying nasty things to herself when she was washing her hair. Then she put curlers on her head and yanked them out again.

"I'm just a big fat tub o' lard, Robert. There ain't no hope for a woman like me."

She hauled out every article of clothing from her closet.

"No respectin' woman in her right senses would let herself be seen lookin' like this in front of a Queen."

Then she started tossing everything out of her costume jewellery box — bright green earrings and purple necklaces and brooches and dingle-dangles flying all over the bedroom. When Robert asked her what was the matter, she sat down in front of her dresser and started to cry.

"I ain't goin' Robert. I got nothin' to wear and I'm fat as a cow."

"Then I ain't going either Granny."

"Oh you're goin' you little bugger — you're goin' or you'll see the back of my hand! This is the biggest thing to happen in this town since ya been born. This is the most important goddamn woman in the world for chrissake — she's the bloody Queen of England! Now get outta my bedroom before I cuff ya."

Robert suddenly realized the importance of the event. He decided to put on his good pants and wait on the front steps until everything got going. He checked up at the sky every few minutes to make sure the day was still hanging on. So far it was pretty good, he thought. Sunny — no wind — can't even smell the slough.

He was glad when Schumacher came to the door to pick up his grandpa. Now if only his grandma could find something to wear. This was the biggest thing in town since he'd been born — the most important woman in the world coming down the street — and he really wanted his grandma to find something to wear. After a while the worry got to be too much so he went over to Mrs. Jenkins', to play with her new dog.

When he came home nobody had remembered to make lunch so he made jelly sandwiches and gave one to Daren. His Aunt Doreen was getting ready in the bathroom and Constance was asleep. Doreen was mad because his grandma used the last bit of water from the rain barrel and she had to wash her hair with tap water.

Finally, in the middle of the afternoon, his granny came out of her bedroom. She wore a red dress with her favourite pieces of jewellery pinned to her front. Robert wondered if he should tell her all the dingle-dangles were pulling down on the top of her dress and he could see the line running between her tits.

Doreen told her she looked like a million bucks, but suggested she go a little easy on the rouge. She wore deep-red lipstick, blue eye shadow, and a lot of rouge. On her head was a curved little moon hat. It perched over to the side. Robert thought his granny looked like she was going to a great party.

At three-thirty the Coutts family started to walk down Second Avenue. They wanted to be there early so they'd have a good place to stand. The train was meant to be in at exactly five o'clock. Good thing they left early because Daren kept stopping every couple of feet so he could pull up his pants.

When they got downtown, Main Street was already full of people. It was a glorious afternoon. Hot — but not so hot that your makeup would run, thought Flo.

The Coutts' found a place to stand in front of the bank on the corner of Second and Main. A lady in a yellow cotton suit stood next to them. She told Robert she'd been trying to keep one step ahead of the Queen. She'd drive into towns before the Royal Party so she could watch her majesty roll up and down Main Streets all across Western Canada.

Directly across the street stood Mrs. Jenkins. She was having difficulty holding onto the dog at the end of her leash. It was a wiener dog, shorter but longer than the deceased Pekinese. The yappy little fellah wanted the popsicle Marigold McConnell was flapping up and down to taunt Lilly Cook's granddaughter beside her. Freda, Marigold's mother, finally just yanked the popsicle from her hand and gave it to the dog.

"That grandchild of Lilly's turned out to be a good-looking kid," commented Doreen.

"They finally stopped the little darlin' from eatin' lawn seed," replied Flo.

Mr. Switzer, the undertaker, arrived on the scene in a tight white suit and stood beside Erica Olsen, the town whore, who was done up tastefully in black. They made a very striking couple.

Sam Hodgenson, Harry Jessop, and Clarence McIntyre somehow managed to get up onto the post-office roof. Flo swore she could see the sun flashing off a mickey of rum passing between the fine gentlemen.

The Baily twins stood in front of the Five and Dime. No wires were coming out of their heads or anything. In fact they looked pretty normal except for the unified smirk creaming across their identical faces. The two girls standing with them were the students from the university who came to do research on the brothers' speaking in tongues problem. The only wires on the twins might have been coming out of their rear ends, because those two girls were hanging onto the boys' back pockets like nobody's business.

At about four-thirty members of the welcoming committee strolled down the centre of the street to assume their places of honour on the platform. "Arrogant bastards," said Flo to the woman in yellow.

The sun was beating down pretty hard but there were still no reports of slough-smell. Everything was ready. Then Eric Meisner started walking through the crowd asking if anyone had seen Mrs. Curry.

At the last minute, Eric got word from the Indian Chief that he couldn't make it. Something about how he'd forgotten he had to go see his cousin over in Spiritwood. So the mayor finally gave in and agreed to let Mrs. Curry on the platform as a replacement.

Mr. Meisner had spent the early afternoon with the old gal and her nephew. They got her decked out in this Victorian dress that the nephew found in the attic. It looked sort of like a long white nightie but her neighbours said it was the real McCoy. It had ivory buttons all the way down the front that glimmered when they caught the sunlight. Eric felt pretty good about the whole thing. She may not be the oldest gal in the province, but at least she gives us a bit of history, he beamed. Unfortunately, the nephew last saw his aunt at about four and no one had seen her since.

Time plodded on. It was already past five and Robert started to get nervous. He didn't know how long people could keep up the wait. Constance wouldn't stop pulling on her mother's dress and asking if her daddy was going to be on the train with the Queen, and Daren tripped over the yellow lady's feet at least four times. Doreen finally got so fed up with the dirty looks, she took her kids across the street to help Mrs. Jenkins with the wiener dog.

Then Flo saw Mrs. Potts standing kitty-corner across from the bank. Alone. She couldn't help admiring how stoic Gladys looked in that purple thing — a dress maybe? No, more like a robe, she decided. And that ridiculous hat!

Oh the poor dear, thought Flo. Breaks my heart. Just breaks my heart to see her standin' so proud and lookin' so ridiculous and alone. She turned to her grandson and said she was crossing the street to stand with her good friend Gladys.

Robert was left with the lady in yellow. He began to sweat really bad. This queen woman was late. Where was the Queen he wanted to know?

Meanwhile, Alister Schumacher, Will Coutts and Will Coutts' wheelbarrow had managed to make it about a mile east of Biggar. They rested on the prairie grasslands. The gentle rise and fall of Bear Hill country lay rolling out beneath them. Will was hogging the sherry.

Finally Alister found the courage to tell the old man about his poetry.

"I'm writing stuff," he said quietly.

"So you're marchin' to your own drumbeat, hey, Constable?"

"I'm not a constable — I quit."

"I know ya quit, ya idiot, and a good thing too. You were a hell of a bad cop."

"I know that, Mr. Coutts."

They sat in silence.

"So what ya writin' about?"

"Fish."

"Fish?"

"Yah — fish."

"Like odd fish? Queer fish?"

"Just fish."

"Aaah — just fish."

Schumacher regained his courage. "Do you want me to tell you something I wrote?"

"About fish?"

"Yes — fish!"

"Oh flesh, flesh how thou are fishified!"

"What you say, Mr. Coutts?"

"Fish — William Shakespeare — I'm tellin' about fish."

"Fishified?"

"Romeo and Juliet, ya idiot."

"Oh."

"Belly, shoulder, bum . . . flash fishlike . . . nymphs and satyrs copulate in the foam — now that's your Yeats fellah. Then there's Milton — fish with their fins and shiny scales glide under the green wave."

"Pass the sherry, Mr. Coutts."

"So let's hear what ya got, Mr. job-quitter poet!"

"I don't think so Mr. Coutts."

Robert could hear the steam engine pulling in and coming to a stop, then a faint cheering and the band playing a tune. The crowd on the street were frozen in silent anticipation. They imagined the royal descent, the solemn grandeur of the procession over to the welcoming committee, the flowers and the curtsies and the essay.

Suddenly Robert spotted her down by the beer parlour. She was in the back of the open car with her husband Prince Phillip. And she was getting closer. The most important woman in the whole goddamn world was getting closer! He could see her dress. It was green. And her hat. It was green too! Then he saw her lips — they were red lips. And she was smiling. The bloody Queen of England was smiling! And her arm was going back and forth with her hand on the end of it. She was waving!

The car rolled grandly onto the intersection of Main Street and Second Avenue. Even the wiener dog dropped its little jaw in amazement. "The woman's got such dignity," whispered the lady in yellow.

The crowd was stunned. They couldn't have been more impressed if an African princess had been parading through their town on an elephant. The only sound was the sound of polite clapping — clammy palms barely making contact for fear of breaking the spell.

The Royal Party passed through and carried on to the Five and Dime. The onlookers remained motionless, aware they were watching something they would never see again. This was history; this was something they could tell their grandchildren.

When the car drove on past the Majestic Theatre — great name thought Robert — and the folks on the corner of Second and Main Street took their first breath, the lady in yellow started to fan herself fiercely with a souvenir program she got in Saskatoon earlier that day.

"It makes me so mad," she said to Robert. "It's always the same — nothing but silence. Oh, a little clapping maybe. But nobody cheers. They just gawk. They stand on the side of the road with their mouths wide open and gawk!"

Robert looked at the woman with concern as she reached into her yellow purse. "No display of public affection whatsoever. What's she going to think? That we're a bunch of hillbillies? Not even a cheer for goodness sake. She must be very disappointed, poor dear." The woman blew her nose.

Robert felt sorry for the woman standing next to him, but he felt even more sorry for the Queen. The most important person in the world had just driven up Main Street and not even a cheer. He squinted up the street and could see the car coming out of its U-turn by the hospital.

Then she started making her way back down. Past the movie house — the bakery — the jeweller's — the hardware — the drugstore — she was closing in on the intersection of Main Street and Second Avenue. The Queen was closing in!

The most important woman on the planet, Robert told himself. What kind of a welcome is this for the Queen of the World?

The Royal Vehicle coasted to Second and slid onto the intersection. It's now or never, Robert decided. He stood up tall and felt a stirring in his gut as the words flowed into his mouth and onto his lips.

"THREE CHEERS FOR THE QUEEN," he yelled. "HIP HIP HOORAY! — "HIP HIP HOORAY!" And the big one — "HIP HIP . . . "

The car slowed to a dead crawl. Robert looked at the Queen. The Queen looked at Robert. She was sitting in all her openness in the middle of the intersection and she was looking. The Queen was gawking at the idiot boy on the corner of Second and Main.

Robert could hear the silence. And he was sure he could smell the slough.

Then her gawk turned into a confused little smile and the car picked up speed and carried her back down to the beer parlour.

Robert buried his head. He waited for the whistle of the train as it chugged Her Majesty off to her clump of trees. Then he looked for the closest back alley. He wanted to get out of town. He wanted to find his grandfather.

The woman in yellow gave him a mint and said she had to hurry because she needed to get her oil changed if she was going to make it to Lloydminster by the morning.

Eric Meisner opened up the bingo hall so the celebrations could begin. The Baily Brothers and their university sweethearts were the first to the jukebox that had been donated for the evening by the Chinese Restaurant next door. Eric decorated the whole place with banners and balloons and had done a fine job making sure there'd be enough food, pop for the kids, and a little extra something in the punch bowl behind the jellied salads for the wicked. "What a splendid volunteer he is," said Sam Hodgenson.

The welcoming committee were late because they had to hurry off to the mayor's house to bandage his wife's knee. She banged it when she fell over to take her third curtsey. Daren and Danny's little brother trailed after them because they wanted to see the expression on the mayor's face when he found out all his stuff was stolen. Gladys Potts didn't go to the party at all. She just stood on the station platform looking up the tracks in the direction of the clump of trees. She was happy.

Later that evening, Constable Schumacher, Robert and his grandfather sat out on the Bear Hills watching the final light hanging low in the sky. Alister felt he was sitting on the top of the world. It was so beautiful. Could anything be more beautiful, he wondered. Suddenly, he thought he could see someone moving in the bushes at the bottom of the hill — a woman maybe? Picking Saskatoon berries?

"Too early for Saskatoons," said Will.

When she got a bit closer, Alister could swear it looked like an old lady running around in her nightclothes, her long white nightie swimming over the tall grasses and glimmering in the final rays of the dusk. Little speckles of sun, thought Alister — the sunfish of the sky.

Robert didn't notice anything. He just kept picturing the Queen, lying in bed on her Royal Coach. And before she reads her essay, he thought, I bet she thinks about that idiotic boy in Biggar, Saskatchewan, who yelled "Three Cheers for the Queen."

An Alien from the Book of Revelations

Robert and his best friend Danny waited outside Billy's front door. Robert felt as if he'd been waiting forever. He was always waiting.

He waited for school to end — that went on forever. And the *Book of Revelations* — he thought that would never end. His grandfather kept making him read it out loud. On and on it went. Just like the universe.

And now there he was. School was out — *Revelations* was over — the pool was finally open — and he was still waiting.

They were never allowed inside the house to wait. The only thing they were ever allowed to do at Billy's was play on the woodpile in the back. Someday Robert would really like to see what was on the inside. If they ever needed a glass of water or something, they had to go all the way over to Danny's. His mum was great. She was Catholic. They'd ask for water and she'd give them cool-ade. They never even thought about going to Robert's. Danny and Billy were way too afraid of Robert's grandfather.

At least Robert didn't have to wait for his stupid cousin, Daren. He'd gone off with his mum somewhere to live in another house.

Finally, Billy came out the front door with his bathing suit, a towel, a package of band-aids and some thongs. His mum was afraid he might hurt his big feet so he had to wear thongs when he walked around the pool. Mrs. Palmer stood with the door closed behind her and made Billy promise he wouldn't run or splash. Then she asked Danny to make sure Billy stayed in the shallow end.

Even Billy's mum knew that Danny was the leader of the gang. He was the best runner, the best rider, and the best fighter. He was captain, general, and field marshal. He was king. Everybody wanted to be Danny's best friend.

Billy Palmer didn't look like he was eight. He looked more like twelve. He was a giant. His mother worried about his giant body so whenever he got the tiniest scrape he had to go home for a band-aid. Nobody could remember what Billy looked like without band-aids. Billy was the worst runner, the worst rider, and the worst fighter. He always got to be the guy who carried the ammunition.

Robert really liked being Danny's best friend and did his best to follow Danny's commands. When Billy ran home for more band-aids, Robert knew how to be the guy who carried the ammunition and the dead Korean at the same time.

They had to walk all the way up past Ninth Avenue to get to the pool. Getting there could be dangerous. There were cops, robbers, commies and sometimes Mrs. Potts, who'd try to catch Robert on the corner of Third Avenue to remind him if his granny ever died he could call her granny. Robert's grandmother told him that Mrs. Potts had three dead husbands already and was hoping to add his grandfather to the list.

By the time the boys got to Third, Danny was Heavyweight Champion of the World and Billy had to sit down twice to put band-aids on his skinned elbows. Then they ran like heck up to Fourth, because Billy thought he could hear the Hell's Angels revving up their engines in Sam Hodgenson's back-yard. At least we missed Mrs. Potts, thought Robert. That would've been really scary.

Crossing over Fifth Avenue, Robert looked to his right at the convent where Danny went for mass every Sunday morning. He was jealous Danny was a Catholic — he got to go through the gate and see nuns up close. Robert figured over the convent walls were rock gardens and trickling little streams guiding the nuns to statues of Jesus and Mary, mother of God and all good Catholics. He'd seen all those Catholic calendars on the walls at Danny's house. The nuns probably took off their hats and danced in their wild black dresses. Why was he missing out, he wanted to know? Why did Danny get to be a Catholic?

By the time they got past Al Capone and the crossfire blasting out of the two pickups between Seventh and Eighth, sweat was streaming down their foreheads and dripping off the ends of their noses. Danny told Billy to shut up about having a rest or he'd rip open his towel and gob all over his band-aids.

Just when they couldn't stand it anymore — when they thought they'd never get there — they reached the highway. They looked up and there it was: the water tower! With B . . . I . . . G . . . G . . . A . . . R painted in big black letters for all the world to see. Below the water tower at the top of the hill was the pool.

The girls went to the right and the boys to the left. Their dressing room had three wooden benches and bolted against the concrete wall was a long eavestrough thing for peeing in. The three boys could pee in it at the same time. They knew three girls over there to the right would have a heck of a time peeing in their eavestrough at the same time. It was fun to walk backwards and keep peeing. Once a boy from Rosetown stepped all the way back with his shoulders against the wall and could still pee in it. He was champion. Usually the aim from a Biggar boy was bad at any distance.

The noise was deafening — hundreds of voices screaming on a single note. It was the top of the world and all you could see was the sun in the sky.

It was summer — it was hot — and anything was possible!

Back flips and belly flops — dolphins and slick eels — brown prairie bodies flapping through the waves. The high diving board sticking its tongue out at the Saskatchewan plains.

THERE'S NO SUCH THING AS WINTER — SO TAKE THAT AND SHOVE IT UP YOUR FORTY BELOW WINTER PRAIRIE ASS!

Get out and jump in, get out and jump in, get out and jump in.

Only the teenage boys sitting on the bleachers were still. They didn't want to disturb the towels laying strategically across their swimming trunks as they marvelled at how much their girlfriends' tits had grown over the winter. As far as they were concerned they had the best seats in the house in the best place on the planet.

The lovely lifesavers paid more attention to whistles from the viewers' gallery than to little Biggar brats dive-bombing the heads of unsuspecting victims.

Boys and girls thrashed about the pool like a bunch of holy-rollers having a mass baptism. It was electric. It was crazy. It was the miracle of summer.

Get out and jump in, get out and jump in, get out and jump in.

When the three boys stepped out of the dressing room, the smell of the water inflated them with courage. Danny headed straight for the diving board and confirmed his leadership by executing one and a half flip plunges before the envious masses, Robert swam lap after exhausting lap, and big Billy, terrified by the actual substance in the concrete hole, just kept running bravely around the perimeter and tripping over his thongs.

One boy, a nasty little bugger from Sixth Avenue, would scream to high heaven as he dove off the high diving board through to the bottom — and then not come up. A lifeguard would blow her whistle and the high screeching pitch of the pool would come to a stop, everyone waiting for the boy to rocket back to the surface. Just before the lifeguards were able to remember what exactly they'd learned on that weekend lifesaving seminar in May, he'd burst through, his long arm penetrating the dry hot sky.

"I'VE LOST MY GLASS EYE," he'd scream. "I'VE LOST MY GLASS EYE!"

And he'd flash his eyeless vacant socket at the lifeguards.

"HE'S LOST HIS GLASS EYE. IT'S IN THE POOL — THERE'S A GLASS EYE AT THE BOTTOM OF THE POOL!"

Then the boy would dive down again — everyone glued to the horror of the event — waiting — waiting for the worst.

Once more he'd spring up through the waves, his hand victorious in the ruthless sky. "I FOUND MY GLASS EYE. I FOUND MY GLASS EYE!"

He'd open his clenched little fist and there it would be, displayed in all its gory glory. He'd done it before and he'd do it again and he loved the summertime.

Get out and jump in, get out and jump in, get out and jump in.

THERE IS NO SUCH THING AS WINTER!

Someone would get sunstroke and someone would puke, every afternoon until the pool was cleared at five.

The three boys spent all their afternoons at the pool. Some mornings they'd travel the ditches along dirt roads looking for bottles. They'd hand over burlap sacks full of beer bottles, orange crush, ginger ale, and coke bottles to the man down at the drugstore and walk out, pockets bulging with nickels. Other mornings they'd spend killing the enemy parachuters who'd infiltrated the fairgrounds during the night. It was hard to tell the difference between the good guys and the bad guys because they were all so dusty. So they killed them all just to be safe — just as Danny commanded.

The sun raged down and their bodies turned dark brown. The weeks passed.

Billy was the first to skip going to the pool one afternoon. Then Robert. It was too hot. Billy wanted to stay home in the shade of his secret house. And Robert just didn't feel like doing the long trek up the hill every day. It was too sweaty. Anyway, summer was starting to last forever. Danny began to wonder if Robert was good enough to be a best friend.

Then a kid named Ron came to town to visit his relatives for a few weeks. He used to see Danny at mass when he came in from his farm on Sunday mornings. He wanted to be Danny's best friend so he tried to impress him with all the stuff he knew.

He took Danny, Billy and Robert to the old garage by the highway and showed them a car that was smashed up. The roof of the car had been sliced away. Ron said it happened about twenty miles south of Biggar right by his farm. The man and woman who were sitting in the front seat were decapitated, he told them. Their heads landed in front of his farm and rolled down the road to his porch. When the show-off farmer boy explained to Billy what "decapitated" meant, Billy threw up in an old tire.

And then he told them about this cousin he had. She was sitting in the back seat of his uncle's car and the door swung open and she fell out, rolled into a ditch, and became a vegetable.

Billy went home to be close to his band-aids. Robert stood looking at the car and worried about those poor heads and the vegetable. And Danny went off to be best friends with Ron.

Robert decided he didn't want a best friend anyway. He didn't want any friends. His grandpa didn't have any friends. He was just going to wander the back alleys and think about stuff.

On a Friday in early August it was Fairgrounds Day. Danny and Ron came running over to Robert to say that the priest had just spoken to the Pope. The Pope! He telephoned him from the convent and got him right there in Vatican City. Danny said he was going to the fairgrounds that night with Ron and even though it was Friday night he was gonna eat hot dogs. Usually Catholic kids only get to eat fish on Fridays, but the Pope said to the priest it was okay if the Catholic kids in Biggar, Saskatchewan, who were lucky enough to be Catholics, ate hot dogs on this one Friday night because it was

Fairgrounds Day. So he was having hot dogs — not fish — down at the fairgrounds. The Pope said!

Robert began to hate the nuns with their stupid little black dressing gowns and their stupid little rock-garden statues of their Christly Jesus.

The sun and sky pressed down on Robert's head. He kept his eyes squeezed tight and wandered back lanes looking at people's gardens and thinking. He didn't like to stay at home. His grandmother just chewed the inside of her lip and read old *True Romance* magazines, complaining about the heat. She didn't even read anyone's tea leaves. And he didn't want to follow his grandfather and his wheelbarrow; he just went off to the beer parlour or out to a field somewhere to be naked and lie in the tall grass.

Robert was by himself and that was that. Just like his grandparents, he didn't belong to anything. Not a club or anything. He didn't even go to church.

He figured everyone in his family were aliens. His grandparents were pretty weird. And his mother only came to see him once a year. She probably had to come so she could plant electric stuff in his head when he was asleep. She was probably trying to program him to take over the world, and his grandpa was probably getting him to read the *Revelations* so he'd know the signs and be ready for when it was time to take over the world. And his father probably wasn't dead. He probably didn't have a father. He was probably born out of an alien robot or something weird.

Maybe the *Book of Revelations* is a place floating around out there in the universe? Maybe that's where I was born, he thought. And that's why I got to learn all that stuff — like a secret code. Maybe I'm an alien from the *Book of Revelations?*

Robert figured he didn't need friends. He was just gonna take over the world.

He thought a lot about the stuff his grandpa told him — and about the *Book*. He wondered if those decapitated heads would be cut off their bodies forever. He knew there was no concrete block out there at the end of everything; there was nothing but forever. That's what his grandpa said. So if you were a cut-off head out there in the universe and going on forever, how would you even know if you were getting anywhere, he wondered. You'd just keep on going. No signs or anything to tell you where you were going or when you were going to get there — because you never were.

And if you didn't know where you're going — if you're just going and going and going — why go there in the first place? There's nothing there. Just forever. God wouldn't even be out there. He's supposed to be out there at the end of everything, but you never get there. So how can there be a God?

I wish I was a Catholic, he thought. Danny probably knows. Maybe I should phone the Pope.

Days passed and the back alleys went on forever. The sun was so heavy on his head he had to wear a hat.

At night he'd convince himself he wasn't going to open his eyes when he woke up in the morning. He was going to keep them closed all day so he could see what it was like to be his grandfather. But in the morning his eyes would pop open and he'd have to wait until the next morning. Then he thought he'd develop secret powers like his grandmother. She was good at knowing what was going to happen. She already told him he had a gift — and a guardian angel. That was probably a clue about how he came from the *Book* but he was too young and stupid to figure it out.

Robert kept walking the back alleys. He'd blur his eyes over by trying to look sideways without turning his head. Pretty soon he could tell what kind of winter people were going to have just by the size of their blurry lettuce. That was good. He kept hoping his guardian angel would decide to fly by. But it never did. Sometimes his dead father would walk with him looking for his mother. But not the scarlet bird.

Then he got worried.

What if he wasn't from the *Book of Revelations* after all? What if he was just a boring boy who wasn't from anywhere and never got to be part of anything? He knew he'd never get to have a best friend again that was for sure. He'd probably walk up and down back alleys forever. And it would go on and on and he'd keep thinking about things and he'd never figure anything out and then he'd be old.

He hated thinking. He was fed up with thinking; it was too hot to think. The stupid sun was going on forever. Just like the stupid summer was going on forever. He just wanted to pull the stupid sun right out of the stupid summer and make it take a rest.

One night it rained really hard and that was great. The next morning he found himself on the outskirts of town. He met a girl who was poor and lived in a house almost as bad as his house. Her eyes never looked straight at him. They went sideways or sometimes inside. She made him feel funny. Sometimes it was hard to breathe when he looked at her.

This girl had a big rain barrel behind a shed in the back of her yard. She invited him to go into the rain barrel with her. So they would take off all their clothes and climb in. Their bodies would slip and slide together like two wet ponies. Robert liked that place in the universe. He forgot about forever.

When the girl's mother came out to the back one day and found her daughter slipping around naked in a rain barrel with that Will Coutts' grandson, she yelled for a long time. Robert's grandpa had thrown her out of one of his apartments when she couldn't pay the rent. She said she hated his grandpa's guts and Robert was never allowed to play in that rain barrel again.

So he wandered some more back alleys and tried to figure out how he could join another rain barrel club.

One day Danny found him out behind the Five and Dime looking at all the neat stuff in the garbage. Ron had gone home to help with the harvesting and Danny was bored. He told Robert if they wanted to go to the pool again before summer was over he'd better get his ass in gear. So they went over and tried to coax Billy away from his mother.

During the last week of August, the pool was packed. Every kid in town was there, making darn sure to get in as much fun as they could before school started again in the fall.

The lifeguards were ready for summer to end. It was still so hot and they were tired of watching little Biggar brats all day. The main troublemaker was this new boy who only started coming to the pool in August. He couldn't swim. Didn't even try. He'd just sit with his feet dangling in the deep end and whine to the lifeguards that someone was going to push him in. The lifeguards would tell him to get over to the shallow end — nobody was trying to push him anywhere — but two seconds later he'd be back with the same whine.

Most of the kids got tired of hearing him complain all the time, so whenever the lifeguards weren't looking, they did it. They pushed him in. And this kid liked it. So he got pushed a lot.

Robert and Danny went to the pool every day during that last week. They didn't call on Billy anymore. He was always tired. Sometimes his mum didn't even answer the door.

They didn't play much either. They just walked up the hill. Robert knew Ron was still Danny's best friend even though he was back on his stupid farm. Let them be dumb best friends, he decided. I'm not even going to tell Danny I come from the *Book*.

Robert couldn't stop thinking about stuff — he'd got too used to it. He still hated it though.

Get out and jump in. Get out and jump in. Get out and jump in.

It was the hottest day of the summer. Boys and girls were flailing their arms and legs at each other to stay cool. The pool looked like an ocean storm — water spraying everywhere and waves slapping up onto the cement. The hollering was even louder than it was at the beginning of the summer.

That's why nobody could hear the whistle blowing at the end of the pool.

"Get out!" the lifeguard screamed. "Get out! Get out!"

Dark prairie bodies scrambled up onto the concrete. The lifeguard threw himself into the water. When he came back to the surface, his face was white as snow. Everyone stepped back from the perimeter of the pool. They froze.

"He's on the drain."

A second lifeguard drove to the bottom.

The water was still. She seemed to stay down there forever.

They waited.

Finally she came up with a small colourless body at the end of her arms. Water clung to his shape as the lifeguards yanked the boy out of the pool. Like a large fish, they flung him onto the wet cement.

One of the lifeguards threw himself onto the boy, pressing his mouth onto the boy's open face.

Then they flipped the boy onto the flesh of his stomach and pounded their fists on his back. They dragged him down the cement and threw him over again so that his face fell open to the sky. They slapped their open palms on his flesh chest. They pounded him, beating and bashing him for life under the eye of the merciless sun.

Robert stood at the opposite end of the pool. Everything was moving so slowly. He could see the lifeguards and the boy, but they seemed far away. All he could hear was his own heart pounding on his ribcage.

He rose high above his body and looked down onto the calm and glistening surface of the pool. Beads of sunlight glittered on the water's skin. He could see shadows gliding underneath. He could see into the bottomless pit.

Rising from the depths of the water, faces began floating up toward him. The water turned to blood. Decapitated heads swirled over the red waves. He could see his dead father climbing up through the foam — and the girl in the rain barrel. He could see his grandmother chewing her lips — the pope with his telephone — Ron and the smashed-up car.

He could see the seven angels from the *Book of Revelations* — the inside of Billy Palmer's house — and his mother waving from a boat in Vancouver.

Then the water became calm again and he dropped back into his own body. He looked across the pool. The boy was dead.

Robert looked up at the sky. He expected to see the concrete block at the end of the universe. But the sky went on forever. And the sun was brilliant.

He raced down the hill — past the water tower and the highway — past cops and robbers and Al Capone. He ran down that road as fast as he could.

He ran so fast he had to raise his hands high in the air to stop himself from falling over. He could feel the wind, the sky rushing through his hands.

He ran past dark alleys and wrecked cars and headless bodies, past dancing nuns and Mrs. Potts and her dead husbands. He dug his hands into the sky. And as he ran he could feel them ripping a hole.

He ran all the way down the hill, past the caragana bushes and into his house.

A boy is dead, he told his grandparents. Somebody killed a boy.

His grandmother and grandfather were talking to Mrs. Palmer on the porch. Thank God it wasn't Billy, Mrs. Palmer kept saying over and over. Thank God it wasn't Billy.

Robert's granny held him and told him it was an accident. Nobody killed that boy, she said. It was an accident. When Robert said that he killed him — he pushed — his grandmother slapped him hard on the face. Everyone does roughhousing at the pool, she said. Nobody killed that boy.

Mrs. Palmer kept going on and on about how thank God it wasn't her Billy. On and on. Robert felt like screaming at her that he'd seen the inside of her house and there was nothing there!

Then his grandfather took him into his room. Robert lay on the bed to listen. His grandpa would understand, he thought. He understood everything — he'd tell him about the boy.

Instead, his grandfather told him things happen in this world that can't be explained — that can't be understood — that there are mysteries.

Robert closed his eyes and pretended to be asleep. His grandfather was old, he thought. Old and stupid, just like his granny. He drew pictures in his head of all the children in Biggar pushing that boy into the pool and waited. When his grandfather left the room, Robert walked out the back door.

He'd never been in the backyard before because he was afraid of rats. He climbed over the fence and walked.

Who killed that boy he wanted to know. Was it him? Was it Danny? Was it those other boys? Maybe it was God, he thought. But if there's a God, why would a God kill a boy? What good would that do? Why should a boy be dead?

And thank God it wasn't Billy. Why wasn't it Billy, I want to know? Why was it that boy and not me or Danny?

And since he's dead is he going to be dead forever? Will that boy go on forever being dead? Going and going and going. And where is he going anyway? And when he gets there — if he ever does get there — will he be old or will he be dead?

I hate mysteries!

He began to feel very angry. How can there be a universe where nothing is supposed to stop but a boy gets stopped. A boy gets dead.

Mysteries are stupid — damn stupid.

My grandpa can go to hell with his stupid mysteries. And my granny she can go to hell with her accidents. Hell — that's where they can go — and God too. Hell. Hell. Hell. And the Pope — and Danny. They can all go. And they can go there forever — forever and ever and ever.

Who does God think he is anyways? That's what I'd like to know!

Robert stood in front of the rain barrel on the outskirts of town. He'd stopped walking.

He looked at the barrel and reached forward to touch the round wooden ribs holding it together. They felt so strong.

He started to cry. He cried about the dead boy and the dead boy's mother. He cried about his dead father and about the people with no heads — about his lost friendship with Danny. He cried for Mrs. Potts' husbands and for the life-guards. He cried for himself.

Then he took a deep breath.

He didn't want to think about the dead boy any more. He wanted to go into the rain barrel, to sink into the slip-sliding wet of the water.

Robert pulled off his T-shirt and laid it on the ground. He wanted to forget about forever. He wanted to get wet.

He took off the rest of his clothes and reached above his head to pull himself into the rain barrel.

But he was scared. He could feel his hands in the sky again and he was scared.

He tried to bring his hands down but they wanted to stay there. He could feel something. He could feel something in the universe pulling on his hands.

Finally, he yanked his arms out of the sky and threw them around the rain barrel. He wanted to push it over and for all the water to spill onto the ground. He wanted to push over that rain barrel. He dug his bare feet into the earth and shoved at it with all his might. He leaned into the round wooden ribs and strained with every ounce of his being.

He was scared. He could feel the sky above him. Going and going and going. He knew he'd ripped a hole.

With all his naked strength, the boy pushed at the rain barrel.

R obert watched his mother's jet-black hair blowing into the back seat, her elbow resting on the open window. Then he looked over at the round head driving the car, the boring brown car that was headed for the Rocky Mountains to his new home in Vancouver.

The man with the head had very short hair. Bristly hair. And under his head was a neck. His mother's arms were reaching all the way across to the other side of the car — her fingers drawing pictures on the bristly man's neck.

Robert decided to look the other way. He swung up onto his knees and rested his elbows on the back of his seat. He could see the fairgrounds and the water tower. He watched the water tower until it disappeared. Then he didn't know where to look. So he closed his eyes.

At least my grandfather's finally good and blind, he thought. He won't need anyone to aim the eyedropper anymore. When the eye that used to see shadows went pitch black like the other one, his grandmother carted all the eye medicine stuff into the backyard. "Blind in one eye and can't see outta the other," she hollered over the fence to Mrs. Cook.

"The final frontier." That's what his granny said. "The final frontier!"

Who was going to help him shave now? Robert wondered. Not his granny, that's for sure. Maybe Danny — I should have asked Danny. Or maybe he'll just stop shaving, grow a beard on the top part of his face to match the one growing down from his chin. I wonder why he never thought of that? Maybe I should write him a letter? Except nobody's going to be there to read his letters. They'll probably just pile up and then he'll die and never know I was even writing him letters.

Robert started to worry about Dow Chemical. It was way down yesterday and his grandpa got really mad. He hoped the stupid brown car had a radio; he'd forgotten to look. Maybe his mum would take her hand off the guy's neck for a second when it got close to twelve and turn on the stock-market report. He didn't want to ask her though, because she'd probably ask the driver and then they'd turn around and start talking to him and stuff.

The car hit a big bump and Robert's eyes burst open, so he decided to look at all the threshing machines plowing their way over the tall wheatfields. They reminded him of the pictures of tugboats his mother showed him in a magazine, the boats they'd probably go sailing on when the dumb car hit the dumb ocean.

He smudged his hands on the window and looked at his fingerprints. If he were a crook, he'd get tattoos on the tips of his fingers so nobody could prove anything. But then he'd have to keep changing the tattoos, so maybe he'd just wear gloves. He wondered why the policeman didn't check for fingerprints on the rock.

They were supposed to leave really early yesterday morning, but when they woke up someone had thrown a huge boulder through the front windscreen of the car and they had to wait all day for a new window to come from Saskatoon — so last night his grandmother cooked a chicken. She stirred the gravy with a wooden spoon and cried. She just stirred and cried. Robert knew she was crying about him going away but he didn't want to say anything because he wasn't interested in crying. What he wanted to know was who threw the rock?

First of all he thought it was the Hell's Angels. Then he thought it was Danny. But he hoped it was his grandfather.

The worst thing was saying goodbye to his friends twice — if they even were his friends. His grandpa always said, "Don't believe what you see the first time — always look twice." The second time he looked at his friends saying goodbye he could tell they were already forgetting about him. Maybe I'll get off in Calgary and circle back, he thought.

The threshing machines were getting boring so he decided to look at clouds. He squatted on the seat and stretched his neck under the back window so he could stare up at the sky.

The first cloud that flew over was a big fluffy one. It looked like it was rolling in and out of itself, like the soapy stuff in a washing machine. He thought for a minute he could see Mrs. Potts' niece Edna inside, trying to get out, but he couldn't remember what Edna looked like because he'd only seen her once. Usually she was stuck down in Mrs. Potts' cellar. Then the cloud got quiet and a couple of fat little legs began sticking out its side. It was a baby — a puffy baby — an ugly puffy baby like the one his mum was going to have with the man driving the car. At least they said they were going to get him a dog — probably an ugly dog — but they did say something about a dog. Anyway, when he looked at the baby cloud a second time it didn't look like a baby anymore. It looked more like an ugly dog.

Then he saw a rocket cloud. It was heading straight to the spaceship cloud that was right above the car. When the rocket hit the spaceship, they got all blurry and spread out across a bunch of the sky. Robert could see the bright shadow of the sun floating behind the foggy swirl — like a goldfish swimming in a glass of milk — or his grandfather's eye — sinking away to the back of his skull.

When he had an eye, Robert sighed. Now all that's left is his "final frontier."

He wished he could stop thinking about his grandpa but he couldn't. The more he tried, the more his grandfather's voice started filling up his head. "Eat your porridge — don't listen to gossip — take your vitamins — don't get married — count your pennies — and if some idiot asks to borrow money, shut your trap and keep on counting." On and on the voice went.

"March to your own drumbeat, boy — walk your talk and talk your walk — and if someone comes along and tells ya to walk or talk different, tell 'em to piss up a telephone pole! You got a mind of your own, Robert. There ain't nobody can tell you how to think."

Except you, Grandpa, thought Robert. You're always telling me how to think.

"There's more to the world than you can see from your own front steps I'm tellin' ya — who cares if Lilly Cook's grandchild is big as a house — there's mountains as high as from here to Saskatoon for Chrissake — there's earthquakes and wars and rumours of wars — there's volcanoes and New York City — and books — not just the Hardy Boys — there's books about the great thinkers and the beginning of man —

Africa and the building of the railroad — and no one got a railroad built by listening to Mrs. Potts that's for damn sure — they done it 'cause they weren't afraid to be different. So eat your porridge, do your exercises, don't suffer fools, don't play bingo, and if you do have to get married, marry a woman who can goddamn well cook."

The sun broke through the clouds and stung Robert in the eyes, so he twisted himself around and rested the side of his face on the back ledge of the car. The heat through the window felt soft on his cheek and forehead. The sound of the highway drummed in his ear. His grandpa's voice fell in with the rhythm of the road.

"There's no concrete block at the end of the universe, Robert. It goes on forever. And somewhere in forever there's a world. And somewhere in that world there's you — getting on with your business — walkin' your walk. There's things in the world you can't even imagine, boy — it's all there waiting. But ya gotta look — gotta look — gotta look."

Robert pulled himself up and sat forward on the seat. Then he swung his head from side to side and tried to rattle up his brain. For someone who's blind he sure talks a lot about looking, thought Robert. I don't think he'll ever shut up. When his grandfather's voice got all mixed in with all the other stuff in his head, he got real still. Then he focused his eyes past his mother and the man with the neck. He looked right down the middle, down the long straight highway to the far end of forever. He wanted to be the first to see the mountains.

He wanted to see the sharp jagged edges, the white peaks that shot straight into the sky. He wanted to see their bigness.

And maybe when the car pulled over for gas or something, he'd get out and race to the top. He'd pull himself up the cliffs until he was standing on the highest ledge. Then he'd open his arms like a bird, his head so high in the sky that no head had ever been there before.

And he'd look. He'd stand on his ledge and he'd look.